Happles and Cinnamunger

Mary Francis Shura

****

Happles and Cinnamunger

ILLUSTRATED BY BERTRAM M. TORMEY

****

DODD, MEAD & COMPANY · NEW YORK

Copyright © 1981 by Mary Francis Shura

All rights reserved

No part of this book may be reproduced in any form
   without permission in writing from the publisher

Printed in the United States of America

1   2   3   4   5   6   7   8   9   10

Library of Congress Cataloging in Publication Data

Shura, Mary Francis.
   Happles and cinnamunger.

   Summary: When the Taggert family's housekeeper wins
a trip around the world, her replacement leads the
children into a mysterious adventure.
   [1. Family life—Fiction.   2. Servants—Fiction.
3. Fairies—Fiction]   I. Tormey, Bertram M., ill.
II. Title.
PZ7.S55983Hap   [Fic]   81-43223
ISBN 0-396-08002-2   AACR2

For Sara
with love
and gratitude

Contents

Happles and Cinnamunger

****

The Super Grand Champion
Bonus World Prize

Later Dad referred to that August afternoon as the day lightning struck the Taggert house.

Of course there wasn't any lightning. In fact it was muggy and hot. The pigeons hobbled along Clinton Street instead of strutting, and the yellow dog in the basement of the brownstone next door barely barked when the mailman came. Usually he lunges against the window glass, baring his fangs and yelping bloody murder.

But that was the day Miss Floss was notified by letter that she had won the Super Grand Champion Bonus World Prize Sweepstakes. While Mom and

11

Dad never knew the half of what followed, my sister and brother and I have never been quite the same.

My name is Oliver and I am eleven, which is old enough to admit that there are things that nobody can explain. Like Miss Floss, who believes in lucky charms and wishing on stars and spitting in your palm when you see a white horse, I really do believe in magic. Which should have made the events of that fall easier for me than they were.

My sister, Sukie, is just the opposite. She is so sold on science that she practically measures sunbeams before she will admit it is a nice day. She is also sold on herself. At nine years old, she is just as abominable as she was the year before and the year before that.

As for Alex, he is your ordinary chubby little six year old and really pretty nice in his own hysterical way. The only things he is really sold on are food and his old beat-up teddy bear.

Because I do believe in luck and magic, I was half-prepared for Miss Floss to win a fabulous prize some day. But not even I was prepared for her luck to turn our ordinary brownstone in Brooklyn into a haunted house.

I was waiting for the postman by the time he

came through our gate and reached for the bell. Mail time was the big event of Miss Floss' day, and she'd drop anything to go through the bundle that always came for her. She has won a lot of things that seem pretty useless to me. She says that "winning" is the thing, not the prize. I bet no other middle-aged woman in Brooklyn has as many rods and reels and folding tents as she has stored up in her room on the fourth floor.

She didn't even turn down her soap opera that afternoon as she sorted through the stack, picking out a thick envelope on which was printed: URGENT. OPEN AT ONCE.

Sukie was staring into the refrigerator and making a face, while Alex, who is short as well as hungry, shoved at her knees so he could see too. I might have joined them if I hadn't realized that Miss Floss, who is a constant talker, had fallen silent. She didn't even seem to be breathing.

"What's the matter?" I asked. "What is it?"

"I won," she said very quietly. "I really won."

"Won what?" Alexander asked through a mush of bananas. Even Sukie, who thinks she is Queen of the World, turned to stare around at Miss Floss, who had never whispered in that funny way before.

Mail time was the big event of Miss Floss' day.

Miss Floss shook her head and rose unsteadily. The doctor in the soap opera was quietly promising a gorgeous young woman that she had at least two weeks to live. You could tell the girl was being brave because she tilted her head back so that the tears just hung there, not washing her mascara down her face or anything. Miss Floss didn't even bother to turn the doctor off. She simply spun around and walked out of the kitchen with a sort of uneven gait, the sheet of paper crumpled in her hand.

It always makes Sukie mad not to know everyone's business. She stared after Miss Floss, glaring so hard that the freckles across her nose looked dark and wrinkled. "It's nothing," she decided crossly. "She's just acting like that to get our attention."

"She got my attention," Alex said eagerly. "What did she win?"

"She'll tell us when she's ready," I told them. I always feel protective about Miss Floss. When she came over from New Jersey to work for Mom and Dad ten years ago, they only had me. I'm sure that never in her wildest nightmares did Miss Floss dream she'd be saddled with anything as snippy as Sukie before it was through.

15

"Big mystery," Sukie scoffed, spreading a fold-over sandwich of peanut butter and mustard. "It's probably another set of barbells or an inflatable boat."

"Come on," I told her. "Be fair. She won that powder box of yours with the music inside and the dancer on top. And my instant camera."

"And Teddy," Alex remembered out loud, wiping the last of the banana onto the back of his hand and then his shorts. That glazed look came into his eyes, and he repeated "Teddy" quietly to himself and started upstairs for the nap he insists he doesn't need but always takes anyway.

Sukie put the peanut butter back into the refrigerator. She says she does this because it is a scientific fact that cold food grows germs slower than warm food. Her actual reason is that she knows I hate to spread peanut butter cold.

"Whatever she won, it isn't going to make any difference to anyone," she said as she shut the refrigerator door.

The reason I quote her remark so carefully is that Miss Floss' prize made all the difference in the whole wide world. I love it when Sukie is wrong, and that was the wrongest she's ever been that I can remember in my whole life.

Since Mom and Dad only work a block apart in Manhattan, they almost always come home on the subway together. Sometimes we watch until they cross Atlantic Avenue and then run down to walk them home. On really hot days we just wait inside the house. That day Sukie shot out the door and was hanging between them when they reached the house.

"What's this about Miss Floss winning a mystery gift?" Dad asked at the door.

"That's just Sukie talking," I told him. "She said she won and hasn't said a single word since."

Mom looked startled and went straight to the kitchen where Miss Floss was finishing up dinner. She came back looking confused.

"She keeps telling me to wait until later, but she looks as if she is going to cry."

"You could have grilled her. You're a lawyer, aren't you?" Sukie suggested.

Mom stared at Sukie a moment. "And I could just let her alone to tell us in her own good time," she said.

Aside from being the best old mumblety-peg player and being able to whistle birdcalls, Miss Floss is also a super cook. That night we had chicken, really crisp on the outside but juicy in-

17

side, with a faint taste of orange in the sauce. The pilaf was absolutely crammed with split cashew nuts, the way Alex likes it.

Alex always sits on his hands until Mom takes the first bite. If he doesn't, he starts grabbing at food in spite of himself. Dad and I agree that people who serve things that smell that good shouldn't insist on manners too.

We had all been served and Alex was already shoveling when I realized that Miss Floss had only the barest scrap on her own plate. Since she is usually her own best customer I must have stared at that tiny dab of rice a little pointedly.

"I'm not hungry, Oliver," she whispered, trying to keep from attracting attention.

"I hope you're not feeling under the weather, Miss Floss," Dad said with genuine concern.

Amazingly, her face reddened and she burst into tears. She got up so quickly that her chair fell with a crash as she hurried from the room and toward the stairs.

Mom was up and after her in a flash, with Dad right behind her. We all really love Miss Floss, except maybe Sukie who mostly loves herself. Although both Dad and Mom are professionals at their work (Dad tells computers what to say), Miss

Floss says they are both "babes in the wood" around the house. I had always figured that Sukie and Alex and I would be in big trouble if it weren't for Miss Floss making her home with us. It would be the hardest on Alex, who is really into food.

Since Miss Floss' room is way upstairs, there was no way for us to hear what was going on, even if Alex hadn't been eating in that steady clattering way that would drown out thunder. When Mom and Dad came back they walked in a funny wooden way and were holding their eyes wider open than usual.

"What did she win?" Alex asked. "Did she tell you what she won?"

Dad cleared his throat, which is always a bad sign.

"Well, my children," he began—that phrase is also a bad sign—"our Miss Floss, after entering every contest and sweepstakes in the world for at least twenty years, has finally won the big one. The Super Grand Champion Bonus World Prize."

"But what will she get?" Sukie asked.

"More money than I ever heard of," Dad said quietly. "She's going to use it to make her dream come true."

I gasped because I knew what that meant. One

whole wall of Miss Floss' room is all bookshelves. She has every copy of *National Geographic* published since she was born. All my friends come over here to write geography reports instead of going to the library. They can always find what they want somewhere in Miss Floss' "dream" shelf. (Besides, the library doesn't serve cookies and is fussy about noise.) Ever since she was little, Miss Floss had dreamed of sailing all the way around the world.

"But what is her dream?" Sukie asked.

"A trip," Dad said in a careful voice.

"Oh. Okay," Sukie said. Miss Floss goes on a trip every year when Mom and Dad take their vacations. She goes off to visit her cousin Eva in Baltimore while we go to the Cape and dig in the sand and eat junk food. "That's nice," Sukie said, turning back to her dinner.

"Around the world," Dad added slowly. "All the way around the world on a boat."

"A boat," Alex squealed. Then he realized. "Oh, but she can't. Who will take care of us?" His voice was rising toward a wail.

"There will be none of *that*," Dad said in his low, firm-father voice. "Miss Floss is already crying because she feels guilty about leaving us to shift for ourselves."

"Then she can't go," Alex said, his eyes brimming.

"Indeed she can and she will," Mom said firmly. "It's up to us to make her feel good about going. We'll manage somehow. But I want no tears. She's certainly earned this trip in effort."

"She's probably already paid for it in postage stamps," Sukie suggested.

Alex's face began to puff up. Somebody once told him that you couldn't hold your breath and cry at the same time. That isn't true but, by the time Alex begins to cry, he is all red and hasn't any breath left to yell with.

Just as Dad glared him into a pout, Miss Floss came back with her face streaked and a wet handkerchief in her hand.

"Congratulations," I told her real fast before Alex could let out a yell or something.

"Thank you, Oliver," she said in a subdued voice. She picked up her fork and laid it back down. "I am even too excited to eat. There is just so much to do."

At Dad's questioning look, she nodded. "I have no intention of leaving you uncared for. I will have someone in my place before I will even consider walking that plank."

21

I was pretty sure that wasn't what she meant but I didn't say anything.

"Perhaps I . . ." Mom began.

Miss Floss smiled at her. "Just put it out of your mind. You know as much about housekeeping as I do about lawyering. I'll find the right person and you'll hardly know I have left."

In the chorus of protests about how much we would all miss her, she served that fresh peach pie she makes with no crust on top and soft ice cream instead.

It was my turn to clear the table. While Miss Floss loaded the dishwasher she told me a lot of stuff she had told me before, how her Uncle James had sailed around the Horn to be in the California Gold Rush and how much she wanted to see Australia.

Only as she turned out the kitchen light did doubt creep into her voice.

"You *will* be all right, won't you, Oliver?"

Already there was a difference in the house. The hall seemed darker than usual, and my parents' voices, upstairs in the front parlor, sounded more worried and careful. But this had been her dream, her long-time dream. I hugged her around the middle like I did when I was just a little kid.

"We can't lose," I told her, making my voice brighter than I felt. "After all, weren't we raised by a winner?"

Naturally nobody talked about anything but Miss Floss' trip for a few days. A man came from the paper and asked how it felt to be rich, and she got letters from people telling her that they needed money sent to them right away. But it was August and the flurry of getting ready for school sort of pushed her leaving to the back of my mind.

Some things reminded me. She accumulated a stack of bright folders from shipping companies that she studied while she waited for things to boil. A lot of boxes and sacks from Bloomingdale's appeared in the trash.

"Just a little shopping uptown," she explained, acting embarrassed.

She was running an ad in the Help Wanted section of *The New York Times*. She had clipped it to the kitchen bulletin board. Underneath was a list of names and appointments. The list grew longer and longer, only to have each name marked through with a red pencil.

"Maybe she won't find anybody and will stay here," Alex said when I explained what it was.

"You aren't going to tell me you are that selfish, are you?" I asked him.

"Yes, I am," he told me stubbornly, his face reddening a little at the thought of her leaving.

School was different because Alex stayed all day. Sukie and I walked him back and forth with us. It always kind of tickled me the way Sukie marched along so pertly as if the two of us had turned invisible. She has it on good authority that the Queen of the World doesn't walk a fat little brother to school.

Then Miss Floss flew into housecleaning as if she was killing rats. I should explain that brownstones are big houses, all built in rows with high stoops up to the big front door. Under the stoop is the basement door, and there is a little areaway like a stone front yard with a gate to the sidewalk. Brownstones have lots of floors—ours has four. One side of it is all halls and stairs, with beautiful open railings so you can see across the halls and partway into the big rooms on the other side of the house.

Brownstones are a lot of work, Miss Floss said, as she scrubbed. The windows glistened. The furniture shone like mirrors. She waxed the hall floors so slick that Sukie, coming out of her room in a hurry, slid and fell down on her backside. Naturally I laughed, which made Sukie even angrier.

She hauled herself up, rubbing herself crossly.

"Mark my words," she scowled. "That woman is getting ready to take off and it can't be soon enough for me."

Naturally Alex heard her and began to howl. It was lovely.

As the day of Miss Floss' sailing drew nearer, she began to get very nervous and cry at odd times. We've really always been super good friends, so I waited until Sukie and Alex were off in their rooms and gave her a big hug.

"Are you afraid now that the time is almost here?" I asked.

She looked startled and then began to shake her head and cry. "No, no, Oliver," she said, dropping into a kitchen chair to fish for her handkerchief. "It's just that"—she blew her nose and then tried again—"it's just that I haven't found anyone to take care of all of you. I promised your mom and dad. I may just have to let the cruise leave without me."

"You can't do that," I told her. "You absolutely can't do that. Can I help at all?"

She shook her head and sniffed. "I've done everything I know to bring me good luck. I even had tea leaves told."

"And what did they say?" I asked.

"That I was going on a long journey and would meet a dark stranger."

"Then you will," I told her. "Else how would any person be able to see your life so clearly?"

Actually, the tea leaves had not been that original. It seemed a good time to give her good luck a little shove. Before dinner that night, I told Mom and Dad about her fears and her threats to stay home because of her promise.

Dad nodded over at Mom. "Thanks, Oliver," he said thoughtfully. "You just leave this up to your mother and me."

That night Miss Floss served fresh ham baked in a pastry crust with a wonderful mustard sauce.

"Enjoy," Dad warned after the first bite. "Such food will not adorn this table when our Miss Floss is gone."

Alex's eyes grew round and he sucked in his breath. I almost gasped. What was Dad trying to do, make everyone cry? And sure enough, Miss Floss' eyes filled with tears at his words.

Dad ignored them and went right on. "Miss Floss has launched such a fine search for her replacement that I am sure she will barely be out of New York Harbor before the right person turns up."

Miss Floss stared at him. "But I promised," she reminded him.

He grinned over at her. "I know you promised, and you did your best. We certainly aren't going to let a few days of restaurant meals stand between you and your lifelong dream. But as I said"—he started cutting his roast again—"I don't want anyone to expect such glorious meals ever again in this world."

Alex was still holding his breath and ready to explode.

"And as for you, young man," Dad said sternly. "You had better start back on your dinner unless you want to miss dessert."

Alex let out his breath with a *whoosh* that made waves in the mustard sauce but at least he didn't bellow.

I guess everyone was a little worried at the thought of actually seeing Miss Floss leave. I had visions of Alex all swelled up and screaming, but Mom and Dad had planned against all that. We all went together to the subway, over to Manhattan, and then to the docks. Sukie was fascinated to follow our course on a map she brought with her. Dad bought Alex a salty pretzel just before we got on, which kept him busy most of the way. I sat by Miss Floss, being careful not to crush the white orchid Dad had pinned on her coat.

During her Bon Voyage party at the pier, I took a whole lot of pictures of her with the instant camera she had won in a linoleum contest.

"My goodness, Oliver," she said. "People will think I am a movie star or something the way you act."

"Oh, I doubt *that*," Sukie said. Then even she realized how different our lives would be. "They'll just know how much we love you," she wailed as Miss Floss moved away.

Only after we were all back home did we realize how empty the house was without Miss Floss.

"You sounded awfully certain that you could find someone," Mom said to Dad, her eyes shadowed by doubt.

"We can approach it scientifically," Sukie suggested.

Dad glanced at her and grinned. "We'll even let Oliver try a touch of magic if he can. But anyway, Miss Floss' dream has come true."

He shouldn't have said that. Alex began to swell and work up to a big scream.

"Postcards," Mom said hastily. "She's going to send postcards. She promised."

"Postcards," I chimed in. "Of windmills in Holland."

"And elephants in Africa," Sukie added.

"And those marvelous New Zealand koala bears," Dad put in.

Alex breathed out slowly. "Bears," he mumbled. "Teddy."

We all looked at each other in relief as he turned to go upstairs.

"One crisis at a time," Dad said grinning. "You only have to survive one crisis at a time."

"Tomorrow is another day," Sukie added.

"I wish you hadn't put it quite like *that*," Mom complained.

****

TWO

The Decibels of Dolores

That next morning we were all eating dry cereal with milk when the doorbell rang. When Dad went to see who it was, we naturally tagged along.

The little woman standing inside our gate was not very much taller than I am. She had tiny dark bright eyes like a little bird and her legs were very thin where they disappeared into heavy brown oxfords.

"I'm Dolores," she announced. "I was supposed to have an interview with a Miss Floss at this address last week. I couldn't come because I got tickets to watch a Tee Vee program being made." She cocked her head to stare up at Dad hopefully. She was shouting a little because the yellow dog next door had started barking the moment she opened our gate. "By any chance is the position still open?"

"Interview," Dad repeated, apparently unable to believe his ears. "For the housekeeper's job?"

She had fished a slip of paper from her purse to read aloud: "Housekeeper. Cook. Children's companion. Lovely family."

"Who could that be but us?" Dad asked with a wide grin. "Do step right in."

Mom hustled us off to school while Dad was still talking to Dolores and asking her questions.

"Did you hear how she said TV?" Alex asked. "She came down hard on the Tee and it came out funny."

"I think Dolores means grief in Spanish," Sukie added.

"Stop that," I told them both. "There's nothing wrong with her or Miss Floss wouldn't have asked her to come clear out for an interview."

Mom had arranged for us to go to my friend Frederick's house after school. She and Dad both picked us up there, looking very pleased with themselves. We all walked back to Atlantic Avenue and ate spinach pies and stuffed grape leaves.

"We can't really claim any credit for finding Dolores," Mom admitted. "Miss Floss had talked to her over the phone twice and checked out all her references."

"Aside from looking like a bird, what is she like?" Sukie asked.

Mom frowned thoughtfully. "Very nice, I would say. The only thing we talked about was whether she could get good reception on the television set in her room,"

"Miss Floss always watched in the kitchen," Alex reminded her.

"I gather that Dolores *really* likes TV," Mom said. "She told me she would rather not eat with the family because her favorite Cary Grant movies are shown during the dinner hour."

We all watched as Dad bumped Dolores' things up to Miss Floss' old room. After we went to our own rooms I could hear Alex sobbing softly in his bed. I knew how he felt. It was weird to go to bed with a stranger in the room at the end of the hall. I could hear music and soft voices through the door. Pigeons complained outside my window and I practiced making that hollow popping sound they do with my mouth closed until I finally went to sleep.

It didn't seem that I had slept at all before Alex, his bear dragging behind him, woke me up by coming to stare into my face with his nose practically on mine.

"What's up?" I asked, trying to make both my eyes stay open at the same time.

"I got woke up," Alex explained.

Then I heard it. From clear downstairs in the basement came the sound of the television in the kitchen.

"That just means that Dolores is down there making you a good breakfast," I told him. "Go get dressed for school and we'll play a game."

It was a full hour earlier than Miss Floss wakened us so I had to play that silly board game until it was time for breakfast. I was two gnomes ahead on the third game before Mom finally called us down.

Nobody tried to talk during breakfast. The sound of the television beyond the kitchen door was just too much to fight. Maybe we wouldn't have talked anyway, as busy as we were enjoying Dolores' food. The bacon was just right, with none of those limp little white pieces or hard bits along the edge like toenails. The eggs were over easy enough to have no crinkle at the edge, and the hashed brown potatoes were golden lace.

"What a breakfast," Dad sighed, pushing himself

back after the third bran muffin with raisins. Then, a little guiltily, he added, "And think what a great time Miss Floss is having too."

"It's impossible not to like someone who cooks like that," I told Sukie when we got out of that noisy house to start for school.

"We'll see," Sukie said darkly. "One sparrow doesn't make a summer, you know."

"Swallow," I corrected her. I said it pretty loud because usually she is the one who does the correcting.

Alex looked up at me startled and began to swallow very hard, so that his Adam's apple bounced up and down in his neck. Sukie and I only quit laughing when it looked as if he were going to cry.

As we got near our house that afternoon the first thing we heard was music. "The organ grinder," Alex shouted with delight, staring up and down the street. He has always dreamed of a thin brown monkey dancing on Clinton Street, like one in his favorite book. When he was disappointed again, he asked tentatively, "Good Humor Man?"

Sukie and I both knew better and she said it out loud. With a sour nod at our house, she explained. "Tee Vee," she said, imitating the way Dolores had said the word.

By the time we got to the door, the sound of the

34

television from back in the kitchen seemed to make the glass in the windows curve outward like those round mirrors in a carnival show. A man's voice was claiming a lot of things for a car. When the sound of a motor roared from inside the house, Alex stepped back on Sukie's foot and she screamed as if she'd been killed. Queens of the World do not take pain with much dignity.

Naturally the noise was worse when we opened the door. We walked down the hall and stared at Dolores. She was poised in front of the electric mixer like a bird about to take off. She smiled and I shouted at her.

"HELLO, DOLORES."

Over the din of the television you could hardly hear the beaters whirling in the bowl. The same doctor on the soap opera was talking to the brave girl. It occurred to me that a whole month had passed since he told her she had two weeks to live. She should do herself a favor and get a doctor who could read a calendar, if not a clock.

"Speak up. I can't hear you," Dolores shouted back.

Then Sukie shouted "HELLO" so loud that Alex and I jumped. Dolores nodded and said "Hello" and went back to her work.

"I'm hungry," Alex said to no one in particular.

Dolores must have seen his lips move because she replied, "You'll have to speak plainer than that. I can't hear you."

Just then the buzzer went off in the oven and Dolores flew for it with big mittens on both hands.

"WAIT OUTSIDE," I told Sukie and Alex, nudging them toward the back door.

With three cream cheese and jelly sandwiches balanced on a paper plate, I went out to where Sukie and Alex were slumped on the garden bench with their chins in their hands.

"What about homework?" Sukie asked when she was halfway through her sandwich.

"After she cleans up the kitchen and goes up to her own room we can study in the kitchen," I told her. "It's really healthy for us to play outside until dinner, anyway."

Alex loved it. He could never get us to play with him outside after school before. Suki got out her roller skates and I used the skateboard and the three of us went out in front and played up and down the street. The yellow dog next door barked until his voice sounded funny. Then the street lights came on and Mom and Dad came walking along smiling.

"I think we should tell them about that noisy television," Sukie said.

"Maybe it's something we'll get used to."

"Let's give it a real try first," I suggested. "Maybe it's something we'll get used to."

You had to admit that Dolores was every bit as good a housekeeper as Miss Floss herself had been. The rooms always smelled fresh and fragrant. Our socks and underwear were always right there in the drawer, and the meals were wonderful. Except for the hum of that television from her room nights and morning, everything went fine.

I wondered about Mom and Dad. Surely they could hear that eternal noise too. Maybe they thought that if it didn't bother us, they could put up with it. And they were delighted that we were playing outdoors so much. Privately I wondered what we would do when it started getting cold and wet. As it turned out, Alex was the one who solved that problem.

Bright postcards started coming from Miss Floss. She had won a prize playing shuffleboard. She had met a new friend named Edith who was traveling to visit a niece in Hong Kong. She asked how Alex was doing in his first grade at school. I was glad for once that there was no way to write back to her.

Alex was strange.

I don't remember that the first grade changed

Sukie at all, but it had made Alex into a whole new kid. He seemed to have wandered off into a world of his own. He hummed to himself a lot and didn't answer your questions. Sukie would say awful things to him and he would just smile. And when he did talk, he almost shouted.

Finally Mom got a letter from school that clearly upset her. She changed a court date to arrange a conference with Alex's first grade teacher.

That night at dinner Mom was really quiet until Alex had finished his pineapple tapioca and been excused to go upstairs.

"I wish you had been there," she told Dad wistfully. "I don't recognize the Alex she talks about as the little boy I know. She says he daydreams and won't pay attention and, if he does answer her, it is always in a very rude tone."

"That is funny," Dad agreed. "Alex may be a mite greedy but he's never been rude."

"Maybe he is just growing into rudeness as he grows older," Sukie suggested.

"All the rude people I know have been that way since an early age," I remarked, staring pointedly at her.

"Did you hear what he said to me?" Sukie howled.

Mom was too distracted to care. "She suggested that I make an appointment and take him for a checkup."

"I thought you did that when you enrolled him," Dad said.

"Miss Floss did it." Mom sighed. Out in the kitchen, Cary Grant was angry, slamming doors and walking off in some sharp, foot-slapping way. "Maybe Miss Floss hid something from me out of kindness."

Mom and Dad must have talked to Alex while I was doing my homework. He came into my room and stood by my desk, dragging his bear and looking tearful.

"Mom says I have to go for makeup."

I shook my head. "A checkup."

He frowned at me, still not getting it. "Checkup," I shouted over the noise of the TV down the hall.

"How come I have to go to the doctor when I'm not sick?" he challenged me.

"Because you act funny," I told him. "You act funny and shout when you talk."

"Oh, that," Alex said with a relieved look. Then he leaned his head over and shook it hard. After a minute he leaned his head the other way and twisted a little. When he held out his hand, he had

40

two of those little red rubber earplugs on his palm.

"Those are for swimming," I told him.

"You're yelling at me," he said, his mouth tightening.

"I'm sorry," I said more softly, putting my arm around his shoulders. "You're only supposed to wear those at the beach to keep from having an earache."

"I had an earache," Alex explained. "Then it spread out and got to be a headache. When my head started hurting so much, I started wearing these. It works fine." Suddenly his voice was normal and I didn't have to shout at him.

"When did this all start?" I asked.

"Right after Miss Floss went away." Then the tears came. He leaned on my lap and made a big dark spot of crying there on my pajama leg. He would have blown his nose there, too, but I am quick on my feet.

"Let me take those down to show Mom," I said.

"I don't want to get in trouble," he said, screwing up his face.

"Maybe it will save you that trip to the doctor," I suggested.

"Well . . ." He thought it over. "I guess maybe."

I rapped on Mom and Dad's door where they

went to read after dinner. They listened soberly while I explained about Alex and the earplugs.

"Him, too?" Dad asked in surprise. "I thought I was getting these nightly headaches from working too hard."

"And I thought mine were from eating too much rich food," Mom confessed.

I had to laugh. "Sukie and I decided we were getting ours from playing outside in the polluted air every day."

Suddenly, from above the stairs and through the closed door, we heard a rapid burst of gunfire and a siren wail from the TV up in Dolores' room. Alex began to bang on the door.

"Oliver, Oliver," he wailed. "I want my earplugs back."

"That does it," Mom said, standing up and tying her silk robe around her like a Japanese fighter going into the ring. "I shall have a talk with Dolores."

The house got so quiet that the Queen of the World even ventured out into the top floor hall to see what had happened.

"I spoke to Dolores about the TV noise," Mom explained.

"It sure is better," Sukie said approvingly.

"Keep saying that," Mom encouraged as she came downstairs.

"What does that mean?" Dad asked, looking confused.

"Dolores says that if the sound of entertainment is going to bother us, she is giving notice."

Alex frowned.

"That means she quit," Sukie explained, hanging over the banister. "Good riddance."

Mom glared at her. "We'll wait and see. I will arrange my schedule to take off some days and find another housekeeper. We were all spoiled for too long by Miss Floss."

"We can certainly give Dolores an excellent recommendation," Dad said wistfully. "That poached sole with the caper sauce was a genuine triumph."

"And the pineapple tapioca," Alex added.

"Don't forget the banana cake with the nuts in the middle," I put in.

"And the earplugs," Sukie reminded us.

Mom sighed. "Housekeeping can't possibly be as hard as it looks, and somewhere in this city there has to be someone a little hard of hearing who would love to have Dolores."

That night I wished I could talk to Miss Floss. She would not laugh at me if I told her that there was something magical about silence. That night was like an enchanted cup that filled slowly with one really wonderful thing after another. Slow footsteps passed along on the street in front of the house. Then a rain began, first with just a few widespread drops that thickened into a steady delicious downpour. Even the pigeons chuckled to each other outside on my sill. If there had been a star I would have wished on it. Lacking that, I went to sleep with my fingers crossed on both hands that Mom would find the right person without too much trouble.

****

A Sporting Try

Dolores served her last meal with a hurt expression and the stock market report going full blast back in the kitchen. Somehow the meal seemed like a party, with Mom wearing that rose-colored kimono instead of her three-piece suit and lipstick.

"I told you that first day that Dolores meant grief," Sukie reminded me on the way to school. "Can you imagine how nice it will be to get our homework done early?"

I grinned and moved the umbrella over Alex, who gets enough spatters because he is short without getting it from the top, too. "Alex solved that problem for us all right, him and his earplugs. You're a good boy, Alex."

"What?" he shouted at me.

"Give me those things." I laughed, holding out my hand. "The war is over and you won."

"I wasn't even fighting," Alex said with a confused look.

It was clear right away that cooking didn't come as easy to Mom as it did to Miss Floss and Dolores. By the time Mom got the dinner all the way on the table, the meat loaf was cold and the Jello relaxing into little scarlet puddles on the plate. The greenish tint of the mashed potatoes was too distinct even for the lumps in the gravy to hide.

Sukie took one bite and made a terrible face. I aimed a warning kick at her shin. I only meant to hint that she should take it easy on Mom. I must have hit harder than I meant to because she winced and then kicked back hard. Naturally I dodged and she got Alex instead of me. He yelped and left the table howling and clutching his leg.

"There's ice cream," Mom called after him wistfully.

"I'm not hungry," he called back sobbing, already halfway up the stairs toward Teddy.

"I may even cry myself," Mom murmured after a minute.

"It's not your fault you can't cook. Who ever

heard of cooking lessons in law school?" Sukie reminded her.

Dad was patting her hand. "Nobody is good at everything. We need a housekeeper who is as expert as you are at your job. I don't think you should even worry about cooking. Just buy a shelf of those canned soups. We'll have a different one every night and you will be free to interview people. On Sunday we'll eat out."

We did eat out on Sunday. We also ate out on the Monday and Tuesday following. As Sukie so tactfully put it, "After the first few times, soup is just something different watered down."

By Wednesday we were all hoping that Mom had been called downtown for a deposition or something so we could eat out again. We walked home from school with an October chill pinching our noses and whipping our ankles. We were still a good two feet from our gate when I smelled it.

"Stop," I ordered them both. "I am having a time-slip. I have been hurled back to the time of Miss Floss. I am a child again and the air of our kitchen is filled with the smell of roasted pork."

"Generously rubbed with garlic," Sukie sighed in agreement.

"Sweet potatoes," Alex crowed. "With that thick

brown candy all over." He was sniffing the air like a small chubby bloodhound in a yellow slicker.

Mom must have heard us because the door flew open and she stood there beaming at us.

"Such good news, children. Come meet Grizelda, the new member of our household."

I can't remember if I have ever told you how Mom looks. She is one of your smaller, more girlish-looking mothers. She has a great tumble of blonde hair. She used to complain about controlling curly hair until Sukie's hair grew out stiff and straight the way it is. Since Mom has to dress in such sensible dark colors for her work, she really goes bright in her off-hours. That day she was wearing her raspberry-colored sweater with the matching skirt and a bright ribbon fastening back her hair.

Maybe Grizelda looked extra dark and forbidding because she was standing there by Mom, all bright and cheery.

Grizelda was tall. Tall and big. Not really tall and big so much as long. Everything about her seemed too long—her hair which was caught in a bun on her collar; her nose which almost came down to her mouth. Even her dress was too long and too dark above those long shiny shoes.

I had the funniest kind of hurting when I looked at her. It must be awful to look so big and dark and unhappy all your life.

"I hope you will be very happy here," I said really quickly, conscious that the Queen of the World was standing there with her mouth open and Alex had grabbed me round the middle with a grasp of iron.

"That would be nice," Grizelda said, with a frown so solemn that I wondered if being happy was something she had never tried.

"She's a witch," Alex whispered on the way upstairs. I knew he was really scared because he actually turned down Mom's offer of an after-school snack in order to get out of the kitchen. "Can all witches cook as good as that smells?"

"Only potions and magic brews," Sukie told him. "She isn't a witch, she's a sourpuss. That's all we need around here, a big skinny sourpuss."

I could think of something to say about sourpusses but I held myself in check and led them both inside my room and shut the door.

"Now, listen, you two," I began firmly. "We really have to make a go of it this time. You saw Miss Floss' last card. She's only in Greece and that's not even halfway around the world. Things have to settle down around here, or we live on soup with no clean socks that match."

"Maybe I could learn to like a sourpuss," Alex said soberly. "I've never tried before. Just as long as she's not a witch."

Before I could answer, a faint, high, blood-curdling sound came muffled through my window. Alex's eyes widened until there was white all around the color like a blue fried egg. "What was that?" he asked in a terrified whisper.

"Only the big yellow dog next door," Sukie said, giving me a wise look. "Howling at the moon, I'd say."

"There isn't any moon right after school," Alex said. Then he turned suspicious. "Do dogs howl like that at witches?"

"Ask your brother," Sukie said haughtily. "He's the expert on everything." Then she slammed out of my room, leaving Alex standing there for me to reassure.

That dinner was as good as it smelled. Grizelda didn't look any brighter or any happier than she had at first glance, but I am not so particular when I am well fed.

The wind grew whippy with autumn. Darkness

began to stay later and later in the morning and come earlier at evening. The trees in the school yard dropped their leaves off to drift in the corners by the fence. The trunks of the trees turned darker, like black fingers against the pale, colorless sky.

On the surface, everything in our house was going along all right. The meals were on time and really delicious. The laundry was always put away and the rooms tidy. But something was gone from the house. It was gaiety. I finally decided that all the fun had slipped out of the house the way the warmth had left the air of Brooklyn with the coming of fall.

Because Grizelda never smiled. She didn't sing or hum or make happy sounds as she went about her work. She seemed to have a pool of dark silence that moved around with her like a portable cloud.

And the big yellow dog next door howled every night.

"He's only tuning up for Hallowe'en," I told Alex and then wished I hadn't said it.

Because Grizelda was so silent, everyone started speaking very softly in the house.

"It's as if someone were freshly dead," Sukie complained fiercely to Alex and me.

"Stop that saying things about dead," Alex protested.

One of the fellows from school came to look up something in one of Miss Floss' *National Geographic*. He only copied the first paragraph or two and said that was plenty. The next day it was all over school that Oliver Taggert had a witch for a housekeeper.

"It's like living in a graveyard," Sukie complained when she saw Alex tiptoeing up the steps even though there is a carpet there.

"Stop that saying things about graveyards," he protested. That night he brought Teddy and came in and asked to sleep with me.

"You've got to quit saying stuff like that around Alex," I told Sukie the next day. "He keeps getting scareder and scareder. Miss Floss wrote that she wouldn't mind staying forever in Egypt. How would you like to see him tiptoe through his whole life like that?"

"I can't help it," Sukie wailed. "I've really tried and I can't help it. How can anyone be so quiet if they are really alive? Remember that nice banging when Miss Floss put the pots away in the pantry? Remember that great clitter and clatter when she loaded the dishwasher? I can't stand the silence. All the noise that Grizelda doesn't make is boiling around inside me like a big whirlwind."

I might have given her one of those "Cool it" lectures if I hadn't happened to look at her. She had big tears balanced there on her lower lashes like the girl in the soap opera. The Queen of the World was about to cry. Instead of feeling happy about it, I hurt somehow. It makes you feel silly to pat your sister's hand but I did it.

"It can't get any worse," I told her. "So it's just got to get better."

That time I was wrong.

Grizelda had been keeping house for us for about three weeks when she decided to do a little better job. She began on the closet downstairs which has always seemed very friendly. She got big square boxes from somewhere and put heavy black paper on them. Then she lettered them with white letters: MITTENS. GALOSHES. CAPS. MUFFLERS. CHILDREN.

"I will freeze to death before I will put my hand down in one of those black boxes," Sukie told me privately. "Who do you suppose is in the one marked CHILDREN?"

I had to laugh because I had already checked it. "It's stuff that only children would use—jumping ropes, my ball mitt, that rolling toy Miss Floss won

53

that we could never figure out how to play with."

A vague smell of turpentine and lemon juice followed Grizelda's progress through the house. She had a little squeeze bottle of the stuff that she carried in her long apron pocket. If you left a fingermark on the table she was right behind you, wiping it off with that soft rag that she looped around the bottle.

If you took a bite from an apple and let it out of your hand, Grizelda whisked it away. The next thing you heard was the garbage disposer gobbling it down, seeds, stem, and all.

One evening when we got home from school and went straight up to our rooms like we always did since Grizelda came, Alex stopped at the top of the stairs and sniffed.

I stared at him but Sukie gave out a big yell. "*Aaaay*," she wailed. "He's right. She's been doing it up here too."

She spun past me into her room and opened the closet door. I followed her and barely held back a groan.

Sukie was right. Grizelda had cleaned Sukie's closet, and mine, and Alex's.

She had taken smaller boxes and covered them with that same dull black paper and lettered them in white. Along Sukie's shelf ran a line of them: BLOND DOLLS. BRUNETTE DOLLS. STUFFED DOLLS. CREATURES.

"Creatures," Sukie yelped in anguish, tugging out the monkey Miss Floss had made for her out of work socks and red yarn. She hugged it against her chest, dripping tears on it as if it were dead.

"Coffins," she cried. "My closet is full of coffins."

"Stop that saying things about coffins," Alex protested and ran to look in his own closet. The same line of boxes marched determinedly along the shelf, only his were labeled differently: CARS. TRUCKS. TRAINS. BLOCKS. PUZZLES.

I didn't say anything. I only looked at my own shelf and knew I could never bring myself to dig anything out of one of those boxes to play with. Yet I couldn't just sit and watch those two kids look as long in the face as Grizelda herself.

"Listen," I said as brightly as I could, "let's all play some game in my room together. Then we can hear Mom and Dad open the gate."

Alex shook his head. "We would never get it put away before *she* did it."

"Then let's draw pictures and make each other guess what they are supposed to be."

Sukie shook her head. "There's only odd colors left in my crayon box. She threw all the broken ones away."

I was getting desperate. "Okay," I said finally. "It's almost Hallowe'en. We could make plans for Hallowe'en."

"Can I wear your old tiger suit this year, Oliver?" Alex asked, beginning to show some life.

"Sure you can," I told him. "It's too little for Sukie or me any more."

"I am going to be a ballerina," Sukie said dreamily. "I already have it all figured out. "I will be like the ones that ride two horses in the circus at the same time. I'll wear my pink tutu left over from ballet classes and something shiny in my hair like a crown, and Mom's lipstick."

I almost shouted. What an idea she had given me.

"Listen, kids. How about I wear one of Dad's old coats and a tophat and carry a whip like a ringmaster? We'd have our own little circus, just the three of us."

"A lot of good it would do," Sukie said unhappily. "You know Mom and Dad won't let us trick or treat. They never do, you know. What's the fun of having a circus in your own front hall?"

"Think about it," I urged. "Instead of candy we'll pass out bags of peanuts and popcorn. When they ring the bell, we'll have the record player doing a march. You can spin in the hall while I snap a whip at Alex and he growls back."

"*Rooar*," Alex growled, leaping to his feet with his hands like claws." "*Rooar*. Snap your whip, Oliver. See me roar."

"They're here," Suki cried as the front gate clicked. "Mom and Dad are here. Let's go tell them about the circus."

There for a few minutes it was just like old times. The three of us raced down the three flights of stairs, Sukie with both hands over her head like the dancer on her powder box, me with a snarling face and a pretend whip snapping in my hand, and Alex growling and snarling like something let loose from a nightmare.

Just like old times.

****

FOUR

Night of Demons

The happy feeling lasted all the way through dinner.

Mom and Dad both thought the idea was really marvelous and grinned at each other while Alex chattered at them about it.

Only when dinner was served did Alex stop talking about a hundred miles a minute. Then he ate at that speed.

"Would you believe that Dad and I have great Hallowe'en plans too?" Mom asked, her eyes sparkling.

"Hallowe'en is for kids," Sukie protested with a look of astonishment.

"Usually it might be," Mom agreed. "But my

law partners have decided to have a Hallowe'en ball for the members of the firm and some of our oldest clients. It's going to be out in a big old house on Long Island with costumes and masks and everything."

"Bobbing for apples?" Alex asked, putting his fork down long enough to stare thoughtfully at Dad.

"Who knows?" Dad laughed.

"What are you going to dress up as?" I asked, trying to imagine Dad in a King Kong suit.

Mom giggled the way Sukie used to before she got so tense. "We thought we'd go shopping Saturday afternoon and see what we could put together. Doesn't that sound like fun?"

"Not as much fun as our circus," Alex told her, scraping the whipped cream off his pumpkin pie and leaving the pie untouched.

"You kids do have a great plan there," Dad conceded.

"It was Oliver's idea," Sukie told him. "And we don't even have to buy anything. We'll use the old costumes and add a whip and a hat for Oliver. Well, maybe a glittering crown for me too," she added after a moment.

Mom frowned a little, studying Sukie. "I hope

that dancing skirt still fits, honey. You've grown a whole size since I last saw it on you."

Sukie had finished her pie. "May I be excused to check?" she asked. "I'm all through." At Dad's nod, she slid from her chair.

I had been watching Alex and his pie. I always save my whipped cream until last because I like the pie better. I had a whole heap of whipped cream on the side of my plate but my pie was finished. Hoping that Mom and Dad wouldn't notice, I slid my plate of whipped cream over in exchange for Alex's uneaten pie. Alex had spooned up all the whipped cream and I had finished that second piece of pie and Sukie was still not back from the closet.

She finally came back looking worried. "Mom, don't we usually keep that box of costumes under the bag that we collect for the Salvation Army?"

"I think so,'" Mom replied. "Miss Floss always kept . . ." Then her hand flew to her mouth and her eyes widened. "Just a minute, honey," she said, jumping to her feet.

I guessed the fatal truth the minute Mom came back from the big kitchen closet with that sad, worried look on her face. "Now control yourself, Sukie," she warned. "I think I have some rather bad news. That box is gone."

Sukie was still standing in the door. Her face began to swell just like Alex's does. Her shoulders kind of rose around her ears and her hands went into tight white fists.

"*Gone!*" she cried in a thunderous tone. "What do you mean GONE?"

"You mustn't blame Grizelda," Mom said hastily. "She was cleaning out that closet and the box was right under the other things to be given away. How was she to know?"

"Gone," Sukie shrieked. "My beautiful dancing skirt, my gypsy tambourine, my leopard suit with all the spots from when I was only five years old!"

Alex was swelling up for real. He began to shout just like Sukie only he was banging his fists with fury on the table at the same time. "The tiger suit? The clown suit I was going to grow into next year? I was growing fast to get into them. They can't be gone."

"Now, listen, you two," Dad said firmly. "Nothing can be done, so it's silly to make this big fuss about it. You don't see Oliver carrying on like a loony."

Sukie whirled on me in fury. "Why should he carry on? He's the biggest. He gets to wear everything first and we have to wait. And wait and wait and wait." She was shouting again and starting out

61

of the room but Dad called her back.

"Mom and I are sorry but it can't be helped. Maybe it will turn out to be a good thing. We will all go downtown shopping Saturday and everybody will get a new costume . . . whatever you want, just as Mom and I will."

Sukie stared thoughtfully and then came and sat down. "That does sound okay," she agreed. "But there goes our circus."

"Not necessarily," Mom soothed her. "Wait and see what choices you have."

That Saturday was almost like Christmas. It seemed to go on for hours with Mom and Sukie meeting Dad and Alex and me under the clock over and over with somebody always saying they weren't quite finished shopping.

Finally we were through, and that early chill dusk whirled along the street and Dad took us all out to dinner. It was really like a party. We hadn't eaten out since Grizelda came, and there was a man with an accordion who kept coming over and playing to Sukie, which brought that Queen-of-the-World look to her face. It was all right, though. She had been so unhappy since Grizelda came that it was good to see her be her old stuck-up self and happy.

Mom and Dad were grinning like two kids. "What costumes did you get?" I asked Mom the first thing.

"Can't I save it for a surprise?" she pleaded.

"Mine's a surprise too," Alex said smugly, hanging tight to his box even though Dad had checked all the others with our coats.

"Wouldn't it be funny if we all got the same thing?" Mom asked with a twinkle.

"As long as we aren't all witches," Sukie said darkly.

"Witches are great costumes," Dad protested. "What would be wrong with that?"

"The kids at school all say that a witch lives at our house. Nobody ever comes or anything," Sukie said sullenly.

Dad and Mom exchanged one of those looks, and Dad signaled for the check. "Never you mind. They'll come on Hallowe'en for the treats. Then they'll see that Grizelda is just taller then most women."

"And sadder," Alex broke in.

"And cleaner," Sukie added with her teeth together. "I hate clean. I hate, hate, hate clean."

"There, there, Sukie," Mom said, giving her a hug. "Let's go home and try on our costumes again."

Those last few days before Hallowe'en were the most fun I can ever remember. Suki even cooled down a little in the excitement of getting the house ready. She cut out orange stencils of pumpkins and put them in all the front windows so that the light shone in through their smiles. I found a great record to put on the stereo. When you set the machine on the wrong speed, it groaned and howled and was really horrifying. Alex was given the job of filling a plastic jack-o'-lantern with bags of peanuts. He almost wore them out fitting them in and taking them out to fit in again.

I had felt sorry for Grizelda from the first because she was so unpleasant to look at. Then I felt sorry that she was never ever happy. And she tried so hard all the time, only to have everything turn out wrong. With the coming of Hallowe'en, she became clearly unhappy, angry even. She frowned darkly and mumbled "Heathen holiday" as she stirred around the kitchen.

It didn't matter. Mom and Dad left for their party as soon as they could dress after work. Dad became a French king with short blue-satin pants and a sort of ribbon thing at the top of his white knee socks. Mom looked like a princess for sure in her full-skirted dress with practically no blouse to it. Both of them had to lean to get through the front door because of their high, curled white wigs.

None of us ate much dinner, not even Alex. We were too eager to get our costumes on. I had my pirate suit on, right down to the pegleg and the flowing mustache, by the time Alex came for help with his back zipper.

"I guess real lions might get their manes stuck in their zippers too," he suggested with his mouth full of whiskers.

But it was Sukie who had chosen the prize costume of us all.

I have never seen such a perfect devil. She had horns and tiny pointed feet like a goat has. Her tail writhed on the floor when she walked and had a mean-looking fork on it. The eyes behind the mask with the twisted grin blazed at me.

Alex grabbed me around the leg.

"Are you you?" he asked Sukie, a little breathless.

She laughed and leaped in one of those ballet leaps so that her legs were both in the air at once. He jumped back with a shriek. Then she began to giggle and Alex wasn't afraid any more.

Grizelda had finished washing the dishes when we all trooped downstairs. When I started the record with the horrible cries on it, she muttered "Heathen holiday" again and went off upstairs.

Only then did I realize that the trick-or-treaters were running late. It seemed to me that, other years, Miss Floss had answered the door for some while we were still at dinner.

We opened some of the peanut bags and ate some popcorn. The clock in the hall said seven-thirty and still our doorbell had not rung a single time. I pushed back the drapes and looked outside. Everything was all right. The areaway light was on and the candle in the carved pumpkin was smoking in the night air but still burning. Groups of children traipsed along the street on both sides, with grownups following a little bit behind to see that they were all right.

"Why don't they come for treats?" Alex asked, standing on tiptoe to look out too.

"They will," I answered him. "Just give them time."

"How much time do they need, for heaven's sake?" Sukie asked, twitching her tail with irritation. The clock struck eight and then eight-thirty with still not a single ring on our doorbell. "What is the matter with those dumb kids?" she asked, with a hint of tears behind her voice.

Alex plopped on the bottom step with his chin in his paws. "How can I be a lion with no one to roar at?" he asked bleakly.

"What about me?" Sukie asked. "I even have eye shadow on under this mask. I'm as devilish under this costume as I am in it."

I really felt a little frantic. We had had such a good time planning this evening. Everyone had been happier than they had been since Miss Floss left. Now there weren't as many kids in the street as there had been, and I was getting nervous about it.

A cluster of small ghosts was passing on the sidewalk in front of the house and I opened the door.

I didn't have a chance to say all the pirate things I had thought of like "Avast there" and "Shiver my timbers." At the very sound of the door opening, the ghosts all shot up and shrieked and started to run.

"The witch's house," they screamed, running off and leaving their grownups to race along behind. "The witch's door is opening. Run for your life."

"Come back," I called. "Come back for treats."

There was nobody there to hear me.

The clock in the hall chimed a slow and sleepy

nine, and the yellow dog next door howled that lonesome way he does now. Most of the children were gone from the street. A police car cruised slowly along the block and turned at the corner. A blue car passed without slowing down. Then a van with a sunrise on the side went by, and an ambulance, but there were no more children.

It was over. Hallowe'en night was over, and not one sack of treats had been given out from the big plastic jack-o'-lantern grinning stupidly just inside the front door.

I should have thought of it sooner. That gossip about a witch living at our house had not only been whispered all over school but around the neighborhood too.

I asked myself, if I were a neighbor kid and not as brave as I was acting, would I go to a house where I thought a witch lived? Where I had heard of children buried in the box in the closet and coffins full of toys on the upstairs shelves? I felt sorry for Grizelda behind her silent door. She wasn't a witch, we all knew that, but her darkness and silence and cloud of unhappiness had fallen on all of us. It wasn't her fault and it wasn't ours, but still a small lion was turning red on the stairs to try to keep from crying, and the inside devil and the out-

Hallowe'en night was over and the children were gone.

side devil that were my sister Sukie seemed fit to explode.

"Who needs those old trick-or-treaters?" I asked in a bold voice, turning back into the hall. The answer was Alex. After all, he's only six and he had his first costume that wasn't handed down. His tail was limp on the shiny floor of the hall.

"Hey, you, Lion," I shouted at him. "This pirate eats lion steak and I'm going to eat you."

I started after him and he took off running. We chased all around the kitchen and through the dining-room chairs, where Alex leaped from chair to chair like they were jungle trees and he had been a lion all of his life. All the time I stayed at his heels, shouting pirate curses and grabbing for him with my hand that was shaped like a hook. It was great.

Then Alex's giggles and roars turned to hiccoughs and I knew he had had enough or he would lose his dinner. I caught him in the hall and tickled him good and we both fell down laughing.

Only then did I realize that I hadn't seen the devil for a very long time and that there was a most curious noise upstairs.

Halfway up the stairs to the top floor I saw the devil at her work.

I froze to the steps as if I were the statue of a

70

pirate instead of the real thing. I didn't say anything because there wasn't anything anyone could
say. The devil had turned into forty demons and
was flying from room to room through the whole
upstairs.

The black storage boxes that Sukie had called
coffins were all out in the top floor hall with their
contents spilled every which way. There were big
signs painted on the white wall of the hall in something that smelled like shoe polish.

PHOOEY ON CLEAN!

UP WITH DIRT!

DOWN WITH WITCHES!

And at the bottom, the most pitiful of all.

I LOVE YOU, MISS FLOSS!

There wasn't a sheet left on a bed. Then I
glanced back down at the third floor and saw that
Mom's shoes, which were always in a neat row in
her closet, marched through her room to the hall
like a confused centipede of many colors.

"A devil I am and a devil I'll be," Sukie shouted.
"Down with witches."

Suddenly a cold draft of air hit me from above
and I knew that Grizelda was standing at the top
of the stairs. She said nothing. She just stood there
with her long thin hands trailing at her sides and

looked at her clean house. Then she turned and went silently back into her room, leaving a wide-eyed lion hanging onto my arm and a devil standing very still in the middle of that awful mess.

I got Alex unzipped out of his lion suit and tucked into his bed with his teddy bear. He was already slipping into sleep by the time I shut his door. Together Sukie and I pushed enough of the mess aside that we could lie on our stomachs in the hall outside Mom and Dad's room and listen for them to let themselves in downstairs. When they go out at night they always use the high stoop and the big double front doors on the parlor floor instead of the basement when they come home.

For a while Grizelda rustled around in her room up above. Then we heard her banging a little as she came downstairs. We drew back in the shadows as she passed. Her hat was already pinned on and she had a suitcase in each hand. The suitcases were dark like her coat and hat and were fastened with giant leather straps with shiny buckles. We peered down to see her settle in front of the door, staring at it, waiting just as Sukie and I were.

My nose began to run and I sniffled. I felt Sukie staring at me in the dark.

"I don't care," I whispered. "I feel so sorry for her."

"You better feel sorry for me," she said. "I hear Dad's key in the lock down there."

"Grizelda," Dad cried, his face very astonished under the white powdered wig. "What in the world?"

"Nothing of this world," Grizelda said quietly. "It is all of that other world."

When Mom pulled off her wig, her own fair hair spilled down on her shoulders. "I don't understand," she told Grizelda.

"Your child is possessed of the devil and is a threat to such decent folk as I. I will not sleep one more night under the roof with such a demon. You know where to send my check."

"May I call you a cab?" Dad asked.

"No one has ever bothered me on a public street. I have no fear that it might happen tonight."

She stamped soundlessly out the door and down the stoop into the dark of Hallowe'en.

"Which one of them do you think broke under the strain?" Dad asked Mom quite calmly.

I was really proud of Sukie, the way she stood up in the hall in her white ruffled nightgown and called down so meekly. "I was the one that broke," she admitted. "I, Sukie."

We waited in the hall while Mom and Dad made a silent tour of the whole upstairs. I could feel Sukie trembling even though the house wasn't cold at all.

By the time Mom and Dad came back to the hall outside their room I realized I was a little bit scared too. Dad's face was twitching in a strange way and he was staring at the floor instead of our eyes.

"You did break with a bang, didn't you, Sukie?" he asked soberly. Suddenly Mom made a funny little sound, sort of like a kitten mewing. Then she gasped and snorted and began to giggle so hard that she couldn't stand up straight but leaned against Dad, who was also exploding into great gales of laughter.

"Wild. Wild. Wild," Mom gasped as she began to get control of herself.

"Don't misunderstand us, Missy," Dad said in a noble attempt at firmness. He was wiping his eyes and still shaking a little. "You have this whole mess to clean up, every spot of it. But I guess that your mother and I knew that someone would break in time. It was just that we didn't know what to do about it."

"But you do understand?" Sukie asked, slipping in under his arm.

"Of course, we understand. We are just sorry that we haven't done a better job of replacing Miss Floss. For now, let's all try to get some sleep so we can face this devilish mess in the morning."

****

FIVE

Happles and Cinnamunger

We always have the same table in the Italian restaurant in our neighborhood. We always have the same waiter, too, a smiling man named Gaetano who makes Mom blush with his flattery.

"It is paradise to have you back," he said, holding Mom's chair that evening after Hallowe'en. "Why have you stayed away so long?"

"You may see quite a lot of us for a while," Dad replied. "We might just work our way through this menu of yours, one night at a time. Shall we start with the lasagna?"

When Gaetano had left our table, Dad turned to Mom. "Everyone has taken a turn at finding us a housekeeper but me. Miss Floss had Dolores all

76

lined up, and you located Grizelda. It's my turn to take responsibility for the project."

"But you'll have to miss work," Mom protested.

"You missed work when it was your turn," he reminded her. "Anyway, I have the entire weekend to get a head start on the job. In the meantime, you must either eat my cooking or we'll dine out."

Sukie reached for the menu. "After lasagna comes cannelloni," she told him helpfully.

"Thank you for the vote of confidence," he said, with a grin.

When we got home that night Alex had tomato stains on his school shirt and Sukie's jumpsuit looked too tight around the middle, but we were all really happy. The house was somehow warmer and more comfortable without Grizelda's silence there above the stairs.

Mom and Dad got out old albums and looked at them all evening. Alex made me come in and see how the round rug in his room was really a race-track. He ran his cars around it, crashing and banging, with sirens sounding every once in a while and squealing brakes when the cars pulled in for pit stops. Sukie cut out doll clothes and dressed a whole line of paper dolls that she propped along the side of her bed. There were paper scraps everywhere but she was having such a super messy time. She looked up when she saw me looking in.

"Hey, look," she said. "This is my whole class. There is Emily and Tracy and Margaret and Louise . . . and that one there is Caroline."

"You did good," I told her quietly.

She frowned. "Cleaning up my mess, you mean?"

"Not altogether. You just did fine." I corrected myself before she thought to do it.

"Thanks," she said in a little tiny voice. "The doll in the ruffled skirt is me." After a little pause, she spoke again, without raising her eyes. "It can't get any worse, can it, Oliver?"

I shook my head. "Dad will give it a try. The third time is supposed to be the charm, you know."

Dad served dry cereal with milk for breakfast but it didn't really matter because the sun was shining after all that dismal weather.

"Indian summer," Dad said when he brought in the paper to read with his coffee. "The last few good days before winter really settles in on us."

"Will you let me try your skateboard, Oliver?" Alex asked, wiping milk from his chin with the back of his hand.

"You have to promise to take it easy," I warned

him. "Or else you could get hurt bad."

"Just stay on our block or the next one," Mom cautioned, looking up from her piece of the paper. "And wear something on your heads."

Alex did pretty well on the skateboard, I thought. He squatted down and almost sat on the board, but he made it go. I ran alongside and Sukie skated show-off rings around us both, crossing her arms like a Russian dancer or holding one leg clear up and gliding.

We had crossed Pacific Street and gone clear around the block the back way and were on Atlantic Avenue when Sukie suddenly stopped to sniff the air.

"Smell that," she ordered. "Just smell that."

Alex fell off the skateboard and smelled too. I got it about the same time. It didn't smell like some restaurants, that mixed smell of hot grease and soap that comes out in steam. It didn't smell like the hotdog cart that parks at the corner of Atlantic Avenue sometimes. This was a sweet, fruity smell that made my mouth fill up from the back as if I were biting on something good.

"There it is," Alex squealed, pointing to a push-cart that was stopped near the corner.

It was the smallest cart I had ever seen on a

street in New York. Steam was coming out of the top through tiny oblong slits, but there wasn't any sign painted on the side. The woman who ran it was handing something to a customer on a napkin. By the time she put her money away, two more customers were in line, sniffing the air just as we had done.

The woman herself was something to see. She was as round as a dumpling. Her hair disappeared under a rumpled, knitted gray hat, and she had on the most incredible stockings in the world.

But what was really great was her face. She had that kind of face that I used to make with modeling clay. Her cheeks and forehead were very round but her chin and nose were tiny and pointed, as if they had been pinched there quickly by someone's fingers.

Sukie was the bold one. When the last customer left the cart, she walked right up. "What smells so good in there?" she asked.

"Beignets," the woman said in a funny accent.

"Ben-yays?" Alex imitated. "What are ben-yays?"

"Like so," she said. She lifted the lid. Instead of slipping out in little waves, a great cloud of that fragrant steam escaped into the air. Inside we could see a row of big sugar-crusted rolls shaped like doughnuts.

"What makes them smell so good?" Sukie asked.

"Happles," she said.

"Happles?" Alex echoed.

"Red happles in rings," the woman explained. "With sugar and cinnamunger."

"Oh," I realized aloud. "Apples with sugar and cinnamon."

"Is what I said," she nodded, smiling broadly.

"How much are they?" Sukie asked. "I could go and get money."

"Quarter," the woman said. "One quarter for each."

"Stay right here," Sukie told her. "I'll be right back with some money."

"Bring lots," Alex called after her, licking his lips as if he had already had one. He clearly didn't intend to leave the cart until he had a beignet. He stood and looked worried while she sold two more to people on the street. Then she started to push the cart along slowly.

"We only live a block and a half up this street," I told her. "You could just push your cart this way."

"Is the same," she said. As we turned the corner

81

onto Clinton Street, I could see Sukie just coming out our gate. Dad was behind her, watching us come along the street.

He smiled at the woman with the pushcart. "My children are sure excited about your. . . ?"

"Beignets," she said, nodding her head. "Is delicious. You try with coffee. Is heavenly."

Alex, who hadn't been two inches from the woman from the first, tugged at her skirt. "Mom has coffee inside. Can't you come in?"

The woman and Dad looked equally startled. Then Dad laughed. "Why not? Do come in and have coffee and sit a while and we will buy some of your beignets."

The woman's face dropped with astonishment. "Me? Ilsa Von der Nagel haf coffee with you?"

"Oh, please," Alex pleaded, taking hold of her hand. "Please."

It seemed so natural to have Ilsa Von der Nagel sitting at out kitchen table with a mug of coffee between her round hands. I poured milk for us kids and we all ate beignets from napkins. I couldn't believe that anything could taste as good as that beignet when I bit through the sweet dough to the spiced apple ring inside.

"Unbelievable," Mom cried as she reached for a

second one. "I hope you have lots of change, dear."

Dad laid another dollar and a quarter on the table and took another one himself. Then he leaned toward the woman with the strangest look on his face.

"Where are you from, Ilsa Von der Nagel?"

She raised her shoulders in a shrug. "All over. I was born in Belgium but that was many years gone now. Since then I have gone this place and that all over the world."

"Why do you move so much?" Alex asked.

Her smile faded. "Something always happens that I have to go."

"Do you have a family?" Dad asked her.

"One small dog," she replied. "Is Belgian too. Named Pitchou."

"Have you ever thought of being a housekeeper?" Dad asked.

She laughed gaily. "All my life I am housekeeper. Like my poppa was happy fisherman, I am happy housekeeper. I cook and dust and clean and bake and scrub. And knit stitches too." With that she raised her large shapeless leg. "This stocking I made," she told Dad proudly.

Sukie's eyes widened at the stocking. It was made of thick wool in stripes of red and orange and gray and purple yarn in uneven widths and not always the same order. "Very warm," she added, nodding her head that friendly way.

"Would you like to be a housekeeper again, for us?" Dad asked gently.

Her face widened in a joyous smile, then grew somber. She shook her head so hard that the gray, knitted hat fell back, showing thick gray hair the same color underneath. "Would never never work."

"But why not?" Mom asked eagerly.

She twisted her round hands together in her lap. "Cannot say. Always is like that. Everything fine and then . . . come one day and I have to go away again."

"If you would just give us a try," Mom pleaded, putting her hand on the woman's arm. "You have no idea how much we need you."

"And want you too," Sukie added. I looked at her, startled. She hadn't acted like the Queen of the World for a long time. And it just wasn't like the Sukie I knew to say something so nice to anyone.

"You could just give us a try," Dad coaxed. "If you didn't like us for some reason, you could leave."

"Oh," she cried. "Is not that *I* wouldn't like."

She paused. "I have to keep pushcart just in case."

"There's a space down by the furnace for it," Dad said quickly.

"And my little dog Pitchou?"

I held my breath while Mom and Dad exchanged glances. Miss Floss couldn't stand "inside animals." But Miss Floss was in Africa, where she had sent a postcard of a giraffe taller than the trees around it.

"And Pitchou," Mom and Dad said in a single breath.

Sukie was shaking her head when Dad closed the door behind Ilsa Von der Nagel, who had gone off to get her things and the dog Pitchou. "That's not a very scientific way to hire someone. No references or letters of recommendation or anything."

Mom assumed her lawyer look. "There are times when a human being must operate on the spirit rather than the letter of the law and trust his instinct. What possible harm could come from a little round lady like that with such a sweet smile and colorful stockings?" Then she looked around the table guiltily. There was one single beignet left on a napkin. "I can't stand to see this go to waste," she said primly. "I'll just finish it off."

"Halvsies," Alex said sternly.

She cut it carefully so both sides would be the same.

"It's only fair," she said with a grin. "Halvsies."

****

SIX

Poltergeists

That afternoon after Dad stored the pushcart in the
cellar in the space by the furnace, he carried Ilsa's
sea chest up to the bedroom on the fourth floor.
Ilsa carried her dog Pitchou in a little wicker birdcage. He didn't seem to mind being bounced
around like that. He stared brightly as he passed,
his ears a little forward and his paws tight over a
stick in the bottom of the cage.

Mom and Dad fussed at us to let Ilsa unpack in
peace but it was impossible to stay downstairs. We
kept thinking of so many reasons to go see her that
she laughed and asked us to come in.

"No more to dance around out there," she said.
"Come visit me while I unpack."

Alex and I sat cross-legged in the corner to be out of the way and Sukie curled in the rocking chair.

"You be my first company," Ilsa said happily. She passed a tin of hard candy around to us. They looked like little red raspberries all squashed down. After they had been in your mouth a minute, a stream of raspberry juice flowed around your tongue.

Ilsa had taken off her shoes at the door. She stamped around happily in those unbelievable stockings. When she opened the door of the birdcage, Pitchou picked up his stick and walked out daintily to sit staring at the three of us with the stick in his mouth. There was an old-looking blue ball in his cage but he didn't seem to pay any attention to that.

"I've never seen a dog like Pitchou," Sukie decided when her candy was all chewed up.

"Neither have I," I admitted. He was black from the tip of his short wiry tail to the points of his ears, which stood up very straight. He was not much bigger than a toy dog but his face, which was a wonderful cocoa color, looked all squashed, like a little monkey. When he stared at you, his face looked almost human.

"What kind of dog is he?" Alex asked, still rolling his raspberry around in his mouth.

"Is dog from my country," Ilsa said. "Is called Brussels Griffon."

"Does he like little boys?" Alex asked, returning Pitchou's intent stare.

"Not all boys, not all girls, not all grown people," Ilsa replied. "Pitchou make up his own mind."

Pitchou's jaw was a little underslung, which made him look stubborn. I whistled softly to him and he cocked his head at me, the funny notched stick wagging at an angle.

"Pitchou is tired," Ilsa explained. "Later he play with you. He like you to pretend to take stick."

"And throw the stick?" Sukie asked.

Her eyes grew wide. "Oh, my, no. Never *really* try to take Pitchou's stick. Pitchou get very cross. Not even Ilsa Von der Nagel allowed to touch Pitchou's own stick." She laughed and gave him a loving pat.

I sat and listened to Alex and Sukie talk with Ilsa and felt great. The minute she had come into our house with her sea chest and her pushcart and the dog Pitchou, I just knew it was right for them to be there. The others, Dolores and Grizelda, had just been false starts. Ilsa was the third try that would prove the charm. I promised myself that I would see to it that Ilsa stayed, no matter what. Like Mom said, what possible harm could come from a little round lady like that with such a sweet smile and colorful stockings?

While Pitchou slept and we watched, Ilsa unpacked the sea chest and made the little bedroom into her home. She hung pictures on the nails Miss

Floss had left, mostly pictures of people eating and drinking and dancing. The people in the pictures wore strange old-fashioned clothes but they somehow all looked like Ilsa in the face—round rosy cheeks and sharp little noses and chins.

Beside the rocking chair Ilsa set a great basket of yarn with needles sticking out every which way like a porcupine. All the time she kept pulling things out of the chest, she hummed happily.

At last she drew out a giant pair of wooden shoes. She set them on the floor by the door and put a small bouquet of dried flowers in each of them.

Alex choked on his candy when he saw them. Ilsa laughed and patted him on the back until he was better.

"Is my poppa's shoes," she told him. "I keep them to remember him. He was great fisherman, my poppa."

Then she looked around the room with satisfaction and sighed. "Is be so nice if it works," she whispered almost to herself. Then she clapped her hands. "Off to fix dinner now."

"Dinner," Mom cried, as we all trooped downstairs to the basement with Ilsa. "We ate all those beignets and then peanut butter sandwiches later."

"I couldn't possibly eat a thing," Dad agreed.

"Then maybe a little soup for the children," Ilsa said, fastening an apron across her wide front as if she had hardly heard them at all.

"Soup," Sukie wailed, remembering that awful week of the canned soup every night. I gave her a warning look and she bit her lips really quickly to stop her groan.

"Soup would be fine," I told Ilsa, not too happy about it myself.

"Waterzooie," Ilsa said, nodding happily as she disappeared into the kitchen to clatter around with the pots and pans.

We only went upstairs because Mom made us. "Don't scare her away," she warned us. "Let her get acquainted with the kitchen by herself. We want her to be happy."

I played solitaire and listened to the comfortable sounds from the kitchen below. Once when I was finished shuffling I heard the faint conversational bark of Pitchou.

Waterzooie turned out to be much more than a soup. It was like a great pot of delicious surprises, vegetable and meat and broth so thick and rich that I ate three bowls with pieces of buttered bread and extra glasses of milk.

"I can't imagine where I am putting this," Mom sighed as she filled her bowl from the big white tureen for the second time. "But it is simply too delicious to turn down."

Alex got up from his chair and went over to hug Ilsa around the middle like he had Miss Floss. Right then we knew everything was going to be fine.

Miss Floss' postcards changed from camels to giraffes and then to kangaroos. She talked a lot about her friend Edith who was a very lonely lady and had no family to speak of. She was traveling all the way to Hong Kong to look into making a home with her niece who lived there with her family. Miss Floss felt very sorry for Edith who was a "babe in the woods" when it came to taking care of herself.

"That sounds familiar," Dad laughed. "She'd be pleased to see how beautifully these 'babes in the wood' are doing now."

For indeed, if lightning had struck the Taggert house the day Miss Floss won her prize, sunshine had hit it when Ilsa Von der Nagel moved her pushcart and Pitchou into the old brownstone. Alex spent hours in the kitchen playing happily

Alex spent hours in the kitchen playing with Pitchou.

with the little dog. Sukie had apparently abdicated as Queen of the World and just sat on a stool and talked about the chemistry of cooking while Ilsa beat and stirred and folded.

"Maybe even I could learn to cook," Sukie suggested.

"Cooking is loving put into pots," Ilsa told her contentedly. "Is be easy to teach nice girl like you to cook."

When we were not playing with Pitchou or watching Sukie get a cooking lesson, we got Ilsa to tell us stories. They were always tales of her life in Belgium. She told how her poppa, as she always called her father, went out into the sea with a horse and pulled great nets full of shrimp back to the shore. She showed us the dances she had learned as a child, hopping briskly from one stocking foot to another until we all collapsed into laughter. She told us how powerful the faeries were in her own country, and how careful one must be not to make them angry.

"Oliver believes in faeries," Sukie said, eying me with a little grin.

"Everybody believes in faeries," Ilsa said quietly.

"I don't," Sukie told her. "There's no scientific basis for faeries at all."

95

Ilsa looked at her in a worried way. "Do the faeries know that?" she asked.

Sukie tried to explain that, since everyone knew it, the faeries knew it too. Then she realized if she said that, she had to admit there were faeries. She finally just shut up with a confused look on her face.

Ilsa looked at her a moment, then patted her hand. "Better you believe in faeries as long as they believe in you."

From the first day it seemed that Ilsa had been a member of our family forever.

By the end of the first week, Alex had started calling Dad "Poppa," which somehow sounded just great to everybody.

But at the end of the second week, the noises began.

These were not loud nor strange noises, just the kind of a sound that makes a father lift his head from the paper and look around with a puzzled frown.

"What's that?" he asked with mild irritation.

"I didn't hear anything," Mom said, putting a finger in her book and cocking her head.

"It was a noise," Dad said stubbornly. "Something like a fingernail being pulled across a screen. From upstairs, maybe."

"There isn't anyone upstairs," Mom told him. "Did you hear anything, Oliver?"

I listened very hard and admitted I hadn't.

The next time Dad thought it was a small bumping, like something being dragged across the floor.

"You aren't used to having an animal in the house," Mom decided soothingly. "It must have been Pitchou."

That time I stayed very still. I had heard the noise too, and felt a funny little wiggle go up my back. From where I was sitting—the three of us were reading in the dining room—I could see Pitchou fast asleep on his blanket with his precious stick tight under his front paws. I could also see Ilsa sitting perfectly still on the kitchen stool, knitting a stripe of brilliant blue into a huge orange stocking. I knew that Sukie was reading a library book up on her bed and Alex was fast asleep.

But since nobody asked me, I didn't say anything.

The next time a noise came, they all heard it. It was clearly the sound of something falling down the stairs, clattering from step to step until it rolled to a stop at the bottom. That sound came a little while after supper. Dad had been paying bills at the desk in his and Mom's bedroom. He came flying downstairs with his bathrobe pulled over his daytime clothes. He always gets the chills when he has to face the monthly bills. He stared at Sukie and me, who were sitting at the kitchen table taking turns practicing our spelling lists.

"Now I heard *something fall*," he said almost angrily. "You had to have heard it too."

"I heard something," Sukie admitted. "But when I am concentrating on spelling, I don't pay much attention to anything else." Dad was looking at me and I knew I had to say something.

"Maybe it was a pigeon losing his balance on the roof," I suggested, wishing I had thought of something more convincing.

Dad glared at me. "Who ever heard of a bird stupid enough to fall off his perch in his sleep?"

"Some birds are awfully stupid," I said lamely.

"Yeah," Sukie said, suddenly brightening. "Dodos were big pigeons and they were terribly stupid. I read in science that—"

Dad was clearly not into an instant lesson on dodos so he interrupted.

"A modern pigeon could lose his grip too, I

guess," he said in a discouraged tone and went back upstairs.

Later I looked at the pigeons huddled on the ledge outside my window. The November moon rode high, gilding their shiny feathers with a faint amber light. I was cross at myself for making up that silly story about their losing their balance. I had only done it because I was afraid that the noises might upset Ilsa. She had never told us what made her leave all those other places. I must not let anything happen to make her take her pushcart and leave us.

The noises went on for a long time without ever seeming to attract Ilsa's attention. She would be off in the kitchen humming over her cooking or telling some long lovely story to Alex as she worked. But Dad got pretty jumpy—"spooked," he called it— and Mom sometimes stared off into space with a thoughtful frown. That wasn't too bad. Then came the night that we all sat down at the table only to have the dishes begin to rattle wildly in the cup-boards.

Ilsa was serving the salad. She looked around with obvious fear and turned quite pale.

"An earth tremor," Dad said, looking up with surprise. "When did you ever hear of an earth tremor in New York City?"

"Never," Mom said. "There must be some other explanation."

"Maybe a big heavy truck banging along the street," I suggested.

"Big heavy trucks pass along here all the time," Dad reminded me. "And the dishes never rattle."

"That time they did, Poppa," Alex said, "because I heard them."

Then Dad looked down and saw the red onion rings and the wedges of fresh orange in his salad and forgot about it. I noticed that Ilsa didn't forget. She stayed pale that whole evening and, when I was helping her clear the table, she sighed a lot instead of humming the way she usually did.

The strange sounds came louder and oftener. They really worried me a lot. Perhaps our house was haunted. It seemed more and more likely, from the way Ilsa acted when they came, that they were somehow linked to her. But how could they be? I got worried enough to talk to Sukie about it.

"The house can't be haunted," Sukie told me right off.

"How can you be so sure?"

"It's plain silly," she insisted. "People move into haunted houses. Haunts don't move in on people."

"Whatever it is, we have to stop it," I said. "I am afraid it will scare Ilsa away."

"I'll ask my science teacher," Sukie offered. "He loves to give big long answers to little bitty questions."

That next night she came home with this strange word written down in her notebook.

"Poltergeist," I read out loud. "What does that mean?"

She shrugged. "I asked him and he said that was what dictionaries were for."

We found the word right off in the big dictionary that Mom and Dad leave open in the study beside their big third floor bedroom.

"Poltergeist," I read thoughtfully. "A ghost or spirit supposed to make its presence known by noises."

"Are they dangerous?" Sukie asked.

"More just mischievous, I think," I said, turning the big book to another page so nobody could see what we had been looking up.

"But what makes one start hanging or banging around a house?" she asked.

"It doesn't say in here. I'll try the school library

and see what I come up with. But in the meantime, if Dad or Mom hears anything, try to cover it up."

According to what I found in the school library, I had been right in guessing that poltergeists were only out for mischief. It also said that they would come to a house when someone had done something to a spirit or had possession of something that was really the property of the spirit.

"What good does it do to know all that if it doesn't tell us how to get rid of them?" she asked.

I only shrugged.

"Very helpful," she said, rising. "Off to the homework. At least I know how to do *that*."

She was barely out of the room before a low steady rattling sounded from the hall. "What in the world is she doing?" I asked myself a little crossly.

Then I whooped like an Indian. That was it. Maybe there wasn't any way to get rid of the poltergeist, but we could at least keep Ilsa or our parents from realizing it was there.

"Sukie," I shouted. "I've got it. I've really got it."

****

SEVEN

And Doppelgangers

"It will never work," Sukie said right off when I explained my idea to her.

"We can try," I coaxed. "Think of it as a sort of military strategy. Call it distracting the enemy's attention."

"Do you really think of Mom and Dad as the enemy?" she asked.

"Stop that!" I told her crossly. "Look, you've seen how upset Ilsa gets whenever she hears those noises that can't be explained. Mom and Dad are the same way, and it can only get worse because they are halfway listening for them now. If we can keep them all from getting upset, Ilsa might even stay forever. That is what you want, isn't it?"

Sukie nodded. "So you suggest that you and I try never to be in the same room at the same time so we can blame the noises on each other. That will be a little tough during meals."

"Meals will be the hardest part," I agreed. "But if we can handle all the other times, we can blame the mealtime noises on Pitchou, who never comes in to the table."

"Well, it's better than no idea," she agreed. Then she sighed and shook her head. "Do you realize how crazy this is? I'm going to grow up and be a scientist. I can't be a scientist and believe in poltergeists. There is no such thing."

"I know there isn't," I told her patiently. "But as long as we have one, we have to do something about it."

"What about Alex?" she asked after a minute.

"We need to fool him right along with the others. If he got scared, there would be no shutting him up."

"And he's probably baby enough to believe in them," she added. I looked away so she wouldn't see me grin.

The plan worked like a charm. Sometimes I had to add other small details to the strategy. The magic word turned out to be "probably."

When a thump came from upstairs and Dad lifted his head to listen, I would look up too.

"Probably Sukie is moving stuff around in her room again," I suggested.

"Women and girls do that a lot," Dad agreed, going back to his editorial page.

Outside noises were harder. When a crackling against the window made Mom jump and glance around nervously, I nodded at her.

"Listen to that. I bet we're in for a really cold winter. Probably it will freeze everything in sight tonight with the cold making things crackle that way."

"My goodness," Mom said. "I should probably check for mittens and boots and scarfs for you like Miss Floss always did."

"Ilsa already has," I assured her.

The stream of postcards from Miss Floss never stopped. She apologized for not writing letters but explained there simply wasn't time. She and her friend Edith kept finding "wonderful" little side trips to take. One photo came from Ceylon of two little dots up on an Indian elephant. A little arrow pointed to the first dot with the single word "Me." I was glad she marked it that way because the elephant was so big I might have missed her.

"I have to admit that Miss Floss' travel has certainly given her a new lease on life," Mom said happily. "And since your father hired Ilsa for us, we couldn't be happier."

Just then came one of those loud thumps from the hall. "I swear that child Sukie is getting as clumsy as an ox," Dad said crossly without even looking up.

I did. Sukie was in the door with a startled look on her face. She scowled at my warning glance.

"If you think I'm awkward, what about Oliver the Ox over there?" she asked.

Dad laughed. "I can't argue with that. I heard that banging at your end of the hall last night, Son. What in the world did you think you were doing?"

I tried to look vague. "Just horsing around, I guess."

"Oxing around," Sukie corrected me with a giggle.

Apparently poltergeists are just like anyone else. Ours seemed to get tired of being ignored. The days turned into weeks and the strange noises came so seldom that Sukie and I hardly had to plan for them.

Those same days got colder and shorter, and we

spent more and more time out in the steaming
kitchen with Ilsa. Alex even preferred her wonderful stories to the after-school cartoons on TV.

We sat at the table with mugs of hot chocolate
buried under whipped cream. Pitchou waited patiently with that favorite stick of his, waiting for us
to get through so we would play.

"Where did he get that stick?" Alex asked.

"Is a stick he found one day in the woods." Ilsa
laughed. "I went to sleep after picnic. Pitchou very
cross I wouldn't play so he went off and found his
own stick. That was the day of the great beetle
hunt."

"Beetle hunt?" Alex asked, his eyes wide.

She laughed merrily. "Is very big thing in my
town," she said. "All the people leave their house
and leave their work and go out into woods to look
for beetles. My country has happy people because
Belgians very careful not to bother the faeries."

Sukie the scientist, having lost the first round in
this conversation weeks before, simply rolled her
eyes at me.

"We don't have faeries in New York," Alex told
her nervously.

"Maybe, maybe not," Ilsa said airily. "Faeries
are very nice and kindly most of the time. Oh,

there are some bad ones, but that is how the world is. Mostly my country has good faeries."

"And they do magic?" Alex asked.

"Much magic." Ilsa nodded. She was making bread. She flipped the great satiny mound and pounded it and shoved it with a twist here and a tug there till it became a glistening loaf. "They make magic with wands mostly. I have heard Poppa say that the wand of the faeries is carved with great beauty. Jewels are set in it like the jewels of the Queen's crown. With such a wand a faerie can stop a river or turn a man to stone. It could even turn such a pot as that one there into pure gold."

"Why would a faerie want to stop a river?" Alex asked.

She turned to look at him in astonishment. "So it could walk across. A faerie who gets his feet wet in anything but dew can never fly again."

Alex slipped from his chair and went to lay his head against her apron. "We sure like it since you came," he said. He left a whipped cream and chocolate mark on her but she didn't seem to care. Then he knelt and patted Pitchou on the head. With his little stick under his paws as always, Pitchou licked Alex's face.

The poltergeist had been silent for so long that I decided that the whole thing was over and we would be left in peace. Thanksgiving came and went and the house began to get whispery for Christmas. The wind howled a lot at night, as it does when winter comes in. The night that Alex waked me, I thought at first his little whispery voice was only the wind.

"Oliver," he whispered, tugging at my covers. "Oliver, Oliver, please."

Figuring that he was cold or having a bad dream, I just slid over to make room for him in my warm bed.

Instead he shook his head and whispered tensely, "Oliver, there is somebody walking around in our house."

"Maybe Dad went downstairs for something," I told him sleepily. "Maybe Mom, even."

"I'm scared," he whimpered.

"You and Teddy pop in here," I said with a sigh, "and I'll go down and check." There was no way that I was going to get any sleep until he settled down.

It had to be Ilsa or Pitchou, I decided, starting down the stairs. I had only taken a few steps before Sukie's door opened and she peered out at me. I motioned her back but she only got her flannel robe and followed me anyway.

From the hall outside my parents' room I could hear Mom's even breathing and that slow rhythmic snoring that Dad swears he doesn't do.

At the landing we could see that the lamp was on down in the front parlor. "What a goose I am," I thought. Ilsa had probably had trouble sleeping and had gone downstairs to read a while. I really felt relaxed when I crossed the hall to stand at the parlor door.

I stopped so suddenly that Sukie ran right into me from the back.

Ilsa was not there at all. Instead, a short stocky man with a very big chest and not very much hair on top was sitting in Dad's chair reading *The Wall Street Journal*. I stared at him a minute before he realized that we were there.

He was wearing a far handsomer costume than any of us had had for Hallowe'en. There was a lot of blue silky material in it with gold braid here and there. His sword hung clear to the floor. Shiny boots and ruffles at his cuffs really finished it off in style.

"You young people are not bothered by having good manners, are you?" he asked suddenly in a

A short stocky man was sitting in Dad's chair.

heavy accent. "Is your father such a peasant that you have never seen a man read a newspaper before?"

"That is his *Wall Street Journal*, you know," I reminded the stranger, a little miffed by his attitude.

"Well, you certainly are staring," he replied.

"I've never seen anyone read one upside down before," Sukie told him. "I think that is pretty interesting."

The man switched the paper right side up with an angry flourish and glared at us.

"You know who I am, don't you?" he asked.

"No, sir," I admitted. "I can't say that I do."

"I am Napoleon Bonaparte and you are clearly a very stupid boy."

What could I say? I am not used to people calling me stupid, at least not right out to my face like that. I decided to ignore it. "I am Oliver Taggert and this is my sister, Elizabeth, who is commonly called Sukie."

He stared at the hand I held out and threw the paper down fiercely. "Drat," he said loudly.

Then he did the most remarkable thing I have ever seen in my life. He disappeared right there in front of our eyes. It wasn't that he got up and went away; it was really disappearing. Things began to show through him. I could see the lamp where his waistcoat had been, and a small print of Gainsborough's "The Blue Boy" that is hung there on the wall showed through where the man's scowl had been only seconds before.

I watched the space a while and then turned to Sukie. "Whatever that was, I guess it's all over. I'm getting cold down here in my bare feet."

Sukie nodded and we turned to go without a word.

We were at the foot of the stairs when he spoke again. I turned around to look and Sukie made a funny little noise of astonishment.

He had altogether changed and had become really a fierce one. I might have been scared except that once you have seen a lamp shade come through a man's stomach you can hardly consider him threatening.

He still had boots on but this time his pants were ever so much fuller and he had lost weight. A sash of some kind was drawn tightly across his stomach, and he had a great waving mustache. In his teeth he held a sharp-looking dagger. Where his sleeve had been ripped off, I could see a full-rigged sailing ship tattooed on his left arm.

Sukie was apparently too impressed to be scared either. "I sure wish you would show us how to do that," she said wistfully.

He had to take the dagger out of his teeth to talk to us. He looked angry enough all of a sudden that I began to feel a little quiver of respect run up my spine.

"Now who am I?" he asked in a threatening voice.

"I'm afraid I'm not very well informed about pirates," Sukie told him apologetically. "One pirate looks pretty much like another to me."

"Unless there's a wooden peg leg or something like that," I added.

"I'm Jean LaFitte, that's who I am," he said angrily. "I ought to slice the both of you to ribbons. One pirate pretty much like another indeed!"

I was thinking of some apology for our rudeness when the furniture began to show through him, just like before. Pretty soon there was the umbrella stand with the dragon on the side and the front doorknob gleaming where the pirate's red sash had been.

Sukie looked at me and shook her head. "Could we be having the same dream at the same time?" she asked. "That's the best scientific answer I can think of to all this."

I shrugged and watched the umbrella stand for another minute or two. Then I called out softly, "If you're not through, you better tell us. Otherwise we are going back to bed."

When no answer came, we started upstairs. "Why do you suppose we weren't scared?" Sukie asked.

I hadn't thought of an answer before a large figure appeared suddenly at the top of the stairs. This time he wore a wide-brimmed hat and a leather jacket with beautiful fringe on it. He was smiling through this huge beard and one hand rested on a rifle as he spoke.

"Now who am I?" he asked.

"Buffalo Bill," Sukie said tiredly before I could even get the words out.

The figure nodded contentedly and began to fade. "I hated to leave until I did it right just one time." His voice was plaintive. "You can't be considered a successful doppelganger when people are so dense they can't even recognize you."

"Doppelganger?" Sukie repeated carefully when we found ourselves alone in the hall.

I shrugged. "Whatever that is." My feet were blocks of ice. I turned off the hall light. "Tomorrow we can look it up but, for now, let's just go back to bed."

Alex was sound asleep right in the middle of my bed. I shoved him over a little to make room. Off somewhere beyond the window I thought I heard a wisp of satisfied laughter in the howl of the wind. Alex must have heard it too, even in his sleep, because he chuckled a little and nudged closer, leaving me only the barest edge of my own bed.

****

And Shabby Old Elves

Sukie was hanging over the dictionary in the study when I came down the stairs for breakfast.

She looked up at me, keeping her finger on the word. "Doppelganger. That's supposed to be the ghostly double of someone."

"He was a double all right," I said with a laugh. "In fact, before it was over he was a triple."

Suki shook her head. "He wasn't right, Oliver. Look." She closed the dictionary and reached for another book she had open on the chair. "It says here that a doppelganger literally means 'double walker.' It is supposed to be the ghostly double of a real live person. When you see one, it is supposed

117

to mean that the person the doppelganger is representing is going to die."

"Well, it's all right with me that ours did people that are already dead. Maybe that's why he wasn't scary."

"Do you know what I think?" Sukie asked. "I think he's something else pretending to be a doppelganger. Remember how cross he was that he wasn't doing it right? I think it's the same thing that made the weird noises. If I believed in this stuff, which I really cannot do if I intend to be a scientist, I would say that whatever it is pretended to be a poltergeist and, when that didn't work, he tried to pass himself off as a doppelganger. He's a fraud, that's what he is. A big fraud, trying to scare us into something."

"It's something about Ilsa," I told her. "I just know it is."

Sukie nodded. "I also think she knows what it is, because of the way she talked about having to leave here when she first came."

"She can't leave," I told her firmly. "We have to straighten this out some way, but Ilsa simply can't leave."

"Good luck," Sukie sighed, closing the book.

All that day I kept thinking about the poltergeist

and the doppelganger and wondering what Ilsa had done, or maybe owned, that would make the spirits angry at her. I remembered all the stories she had told about the faeries in Belgium. When I think of faeries I always see them with blond hair and little lacy wings. Maybe Belgian faeries were something a lot more solid than that, and a lot peskier.

By the end of that day, I had decided that the thing to do was to face up to Ilsa and ask her straight out. If she knew why they were after her, we could maybe figure out how to satisfy them. If she didn't know . . . well, that would be harder.

I didn't even wait for Sukie and Alex that afternoon when we crossed Atlantic Avenue. I left them and raced for home. I needed to talk to Ilsa the first minute before I lost my courage about mentioning it to her.

I opened the door and ran down the hall just like always, expecting to see Ilsa there by the stove getting our hot chocolate warmed up. Instead I heard the distant whine of the vacuum from upstairs. But I was not alone in the kitchen.

There on the cupboard with both hands full squatted a little man no taller than an eighteen-inch ruler. He was shabbily dressed, and from the back I could see the soles of his dirty feet peeking

through the holes in his shoes. He was so intent on
his work that he didn't even hear me. To my hor-
ror I realized that he was emptying a fresh box of
salt into the sugar canister.

Sukie and Alex were at the kitchen door behind me. Sukie saw what was going on right away and whispered, "Grab him."

Fortunately, Alex was astonished into silence.

I shot across the room and caught the little fellow just as he turned. He was obviously terrified. He kicked and tugged and screamed and made such terrible faces that I had to shut my eyes to keep hanging onto him.

"Let me go, you bully beast," he screamed. "Let me go or I'll turn you into a frog."

"That's the wrong way for evolution," Sukie pointed out from the door.

"A stone, a goat, a tree," the man threatened, kicking my arm something fearful with his worn-out shoes.

"A lot of good it would do you," I told him. "You just tell me what you and your spooky friends are after or I'll . . ." For a minute there I couldn't think of any threat to make. Then I saw Ilsa's supper simmering on the back of the stove. "I'll drown you right in this pot of split pea soup."

The little man howled and kicked harder than ever as I held him over the simmering pot.

Alex was whimpering and hanging onto Sukie for dear life.

"You must think I'm pretty stupid," the elf said with a sneer. "If I told you what we want, you would take it and use it against us. You . . . you human."

I felt my hand turn suddenly very cold and damp. The elf had turned into a very warty toad that squirmed bright green between my fingers.

Alex squealed with delight. "Oh, give it to me. A frog!"

"*Ugh,*" Sukie groaned, jerking Alex back.

Then my wrist hurt. I mean it really hurt. The frog had turned into a heavy beaked falcon that was pecking me so painfully that I was within an inch of letting him go. I slapped it across the head and at once it turned into a tiny green snake. That time it happened too fast for me. The snake was so slick that it slithered right through my fingers, hit the floor with a slimy slip, and wriggled out through the open back door, its small forked tongue darting rapidly as it went. Sukie jumped back and screamed as it passed her, knocking down Alex who was hanging there against her.

I stood rubbing my pecked wrist and feeling like a total failure. Then I realized how quiet it was. The sound of the vacuum had stopped. Ilsa was standing there in the kitchen door with giant tears working their way down her plump cheeks. Pitchou, his stick in his mouth, stood beside her wagging his tail to welcome us home.

When she saw us staring, Ilsa threw her apron up over her face and began to wail. Her sturdy body was shaking with massive sobs.

"What do they want, Ilsa?" I asked. "What have you done to the faeries?"

"*Ooooooooooh,*" she wailed. "And don't you think I would like to know myself? Is good all my life to faeries and they be good to me. I steal nothing from faeries and they be my friends. Then of a suddenly they start to pick on me. I have no idea why. I get good job, they come to pester. They drive me from every place I be happy. I give up. I go home to Belgium and give up."

Naturally Alex had began to bellow when he saw Ilsa cry.

I motioned for Sukie to take Alex upstairs but she shook her head and pulled him against her, patting him instead.

"You simply cannot go," Sukie told Ilsa firmly. "We love you too much. That's the final word: you can't leave us."

"We like spooky things," I told her. "Faeries can come and faeries can go, but we still want you."

123

Alex was crying so hard that Ilsa couldn't stand it. She wiped her face and sat down on the kitchen chair to pull him up on her lap. "Is not good to cry, Alex," she told him gently, wiping his face with her apron too. "Is going to have river running from your nose."

"Promise you won't leave," he begged.

"New ginger cookies are in box over there," she told Sukie. "We have ginger cookies and milk now with no more talk of such things."

She would have it no other way, and we finally had the saddest after-school tea party we had ever had since Ilsa came.

That night Dad noticed the redness around Ilsa's eyes. "I don't think Ilsa looks as if she feels very well," he said thoughtfully. "It almost looks as if she has been crying."

"Ilsa crying?" Mom cried. "Do you children know anything about this?"

I tried to get in there first but Alex was too quick for me.

"Elves make Ilsa cry," he said briskly. "Elves that turn to frogs and birds and snakes that waggle around." He made a writhing motion with his hand very fast. When he did that he hit his glass of milk and it spilled into Sukie's soup bowl and the plate underneath.

By the time the mess was cleared away and a towel put under the tablecloth at Sukie's place to save the finish of the table, Dad had clearly forgotten what started the whole thing.

Sukie and I exchanged a look of relief. Neither of us wanted to try to make a computer specialist and an attorney believe in faeries halfway through dinner.

****

NINE

One and One and One

That night it snowed. I watched the flakes slide quickly down the warmed glass of my windows. I hoped that shabby old elf had the coldest feet in America, walking around making trouble in his worn-out old shoes. I hoped the poltergeist fell on the ice and cracked his noisemaker forty ways. I hoped that vain old doppleganger would be arrested for impersonating an officer and be slammed in a cold, damp jail cell with nothing to eat but cereal with lumps in it.

But most of all I wished I could figure out what Ilsa had done to irritate the faeries, so we could figure out how to make it up to them.

One thing kept coming back to me. When I had

held the elf over the hot soup kettle, the little man had said: "You would use it against us."

What was "it"? It sounded as if he thought Ilsa had something that belonged to the faeries. But surely she would know it if she did. Hadn't she said that she had never stolen from the faeries nor the faeries stolen from her?

Because of the snow there was a lot of extra confusion that morning. Sukie sorted out the hats and mufflers from the mess that was left in the closet when she tore up all those black boxes of Grizelda's. I was sent to the cellar to bring up all the rubber boots. The cellar looked funny somehow, but I didn't take time to figure out why as I ran back upstairs for breakfast.

The cold seemed to finger into the house in little drafts. Sukie was dressed in wool pants and a sweater and Alex bundled up like a snowman, but still it didn't feel all that warm. Pitchou was clearly uncomfortable. He curled by the stove under Ilsa's feet, shivering.

"Can I cover him with a little blanket?" Alex asked. "Or could I hold him on my lap while I have my oatmeal?"

"He has sweater," Ilsa said briskly. "Is very warm sweater I knit for him myself." She was lifting French toast onto my plate as she spoke.

"Tell me where it is and I'll get it for him," I offered.

"Good boy." Ilsa smiled at me, sliding another piece of toast into the sizzling butter. "Is on rocking chair in my room. There on the back. Is red and purple."

When I came down I buttoned the sweater on Pitchou, who licked my face for thanks, then tugged at my sleeve, asking me to play. I pretended I wanted his stick and then sat down to eat before my toast got cold. While I was putting the hot maple syrup on I realized that something had seemed funny to me about Ilsa's room too, but I couldn't pin down in my mind just what had bothered me.

Finally we were bundled up and out the door into the thick white world of the street. Our books had been wrapped in plastic to protect them from the snow which swirled around us as we walked toward school.

Ilsa had given us each a good-bye hug at the door as always.

"Is be good little man," she told me as Alex slid off down the sidewalk. Sukie was right after him but she didn't have to worry. He was skating along on his boots making gray mushes behind himself on the walk and giggling like anything. The two of them played all the way to the corner but I just plodded along frowning. Something had been different and wrong when we left home. For the life of me I couldn't figure out what it was.

The closer we got to school, the more kids there were playing along the sidewalk. I heard someone yell at me but I only shook my head.

Wrong. Wrong. There had been something really wrong about the whole morning.

Then I remembered. Every morning when I leave for school, Ilsa says, "Is be good boy."

This morning she had changed that and said, "Is be good little man." Why should I suddenly be a good little man instead of just a plain old good boy?

And Ilsa's room. There had been something strange there when I went up to get the sweater for Pitchou. The pictures! All the pictures of the laughing, feasting people who looked like herself had been gone from Ilsa's walls. Why should she take her pictures down when it wasn't even a special cleaning day?

And the cellar. When I had gone back by the furnace to get the snow boots.

The kids were lining up because it was time for the bell. Alex was clear down at the end of the school yard and Sukie was in the middle of a bunch of giggling girls. I raced down to where Sukie was and whispered, "C'mon, Sukie. Something awful has happened. We have to go back home."

She looked confused but she didn't argue. "Tell Alex anything you want, but just get him," I ordered.

Within minutes she came back with him and the three of us left the school yard in the confusion of kids running to get there while the bell was ringing.

"This is clearly against the rules," Sukie said, panting a little to keep up with me.

I could see the place by the furnace in my mind as plainly as if I were still standing there. The boots had been in a box marked HEAVY WEATHER GEAR. Then there was an empty space and then the side of the furnace. Ilsa's pushcart had been stored in that empty place and now it was gone.

I kept us moving as fast as we could go in those awkward rubber boots. Sukie was complaining furiously that she needed to be explained to and I kept telling her, "Later. Later," to save breath for running. Alex was so slow that I finally took his hand and hurried him along. He was puffing and panting and lost one mitten in the gutter but there was simply no time to stop and fish it out.

After what seemed a first cousin to forever, we reached our own block. I got inside the gate and then began to pound on the window with both fists. The big yellow dog next door came to his window and started to bark and howl that way he does when anyone makes a different noise. From inside our house I could hear only the hollow echo of my own banging. I got the hidden emergency key from under the chipped piece of brownstone in the foundation. I was relieved to find it because I hadn't used it since Grizelda left.

The key turned hard in the cold lock but I was finally in. Sukie and Alex stood beside me staring at the dark, unlit kitchen. That wonderful smell was in the air, the smell that had first led us to Ilsa. "Happles and cinnamunger," she called it.

And sure enough, on the gleamingly polished table was a plate with a blue-and-white checked napkin over it. I lifted the napkin and touched an apple beignet with my finger. It was still hot. The sugar crust clung to my finger and I had to lick it off or it might even have burned me. I could feel the emptiness of that house like a pillar of silence

131

around me as I read the note that had been written on a piece of lined notebook paper and pushed under the plate.

"DEAR ONES. IS SORRY TO LEAVE YOU.
IS NO OTHER WAY.   LOVE,
ILSA VON der NAGEL"

"Leave?" Alex said. Then he began to hold his breath and turn red.

I turned on him quickly. "You simply cannot cry," I told him crossly. "We haven't time for that. Everybody go get all the money you have."

"I haven't much," Sukie replied.

"Neither have I," I admitted. "And Alex will have even less, but we have to get Ilsa and bring her back home."

Sukie was halfway up the stairs when I remembered. "While you're up there, do you have that map you marked the day we took Miss Floss to her ship?"

She stared at me and nodded. "How do you know it will be the same pier? There are millions of them. At least dozens."

"Miss Floss was going to Holland first. With

132

Belgium and Holland right there together, I thought maybe . . ."

She nodded briskly. "I'll be right down."

When all our money was together, I stared at it in my hand.

"Is there enough?" Sukie asked.

"It has to be," I said grimly. "Let's go."

"And leave the ben-yays?" Alex asked, incredulous.

"We'll be back," I promised him. "We'll *all* be back."

Out on the street I paused in a moment of real doubt. "How would you start on Clinton Street in Brooklyn to go to Belgium?"

"If I had money, I'd walk down to Atlantic Avenue and hail a cab," Sukie said, turning her back to the bitter wind.

"Never let me knock scientific deduction again," I told her. "Down to the corner, everyone."

The man who sweeps out the store on the corner was wearing a big striped muffler that trailed down and fanned fringe all over his broom.

"Sir? I asked. "Did you see a woman leave from this corner?"

"A woman leave," he repeated acidly. "I have

133

seen a million women leave in my time, from every corner in the world. You might say that I have never seen a woman stay. Big ones. Little ones. Happy ones. Cross ones."

"This was a pretty big one," Sukie told him. "She had a pushcart and a sea chest and a birdcage with a little black dog in it."

The man leaned on his broom and laughed.

"You are in luck, kid," he said. "Even I would notice such as that, and I did. She took a cab and, believe me, it wasn't all that easy to talk the driver into getting all that stuff inside."

I stepped into the street and hailed a cab just like I have seen Dad do. The taxi pulled in and asked, "Where to?"

I dumped all our money out on the seat of his cab. He pushed it around with a stubby finger before scooping it up and handing it back to me.

"No way. You could make it by subway and bus maybe but not with me."

He took off with a wet swoosh that sprayed slush halfway up my legs.

"We don't need him anyway," Sukie said crossly, trying to wipe off her slacks with a mitten. "We'll go by subway, just like we did before."

134

"I hope we're doing the right thing," she added when the three of us were all packed into a single seat in the crowded subway car.

"That's two of us," I told her.

"Three," Alex said. "I still think we should have brought along the ben-yays."

****

TEN

Bon Voyage

That whole morning was ridiculous. If I had taken time to think about what we were doing, I wouldn't have had the courage. As it was, Sukie was the only reason it worked. She remembered. I must have been excited the day Miss Floss left because it hadn't registered on me just how we had traveled to the pier.

"You follow my lead or I won't go," Sukie insisted as we got off the train the same place we had before.

The snow was still swirling around when we climbed up to the street, and she got this funny look on her face.

"Now what?" I asked.

"This is where Dad called the cab," she told me in a funny choked voice.

"I have to go to the bathroom," Alex announced, dramatizing this statement with that little dance he does.

Fortunately, the man in the store where I asked had a little kid like Alex. "Not as fat as him," he told me, as he showed me the way to the washroom.

Then, miracle of miracles, he knew the way to the pier where the ships left for Holland. "Beauties, they are. But aren't you kids a little young for a cruise?"

"We're seeing someone off," Sukie explained. Then she winked at me. "Off the ship," she said later, "not off on a cruise. Get it?"

I smiled as hard as I could under the circumstances. When the Queen of the World has mud all over her good pants and can still make jokes, the least I can do is act amused.

There was plenty of money for the bus. We got off at the Hudson River when the bus driver said to. There were so many lines of taxis he said there had to be several ships leaving about then. Through the whirling snow we could see the wag of a boom swaying high above a ship.

"Everyone hang on," I ordered, setting out through the milling crowd with Sukie and Alex in tow. I didn't even look at the faces of the people I ran into because I didn't have time to apologize. The gangplank on the ship was down and people were walking back and forth with a carefree, holiday sort of look. Women were carrying flowers and there were even some children with tiny flags in their mittened fists.

Porters were passing with luggage on rolling carts. I ran after one and tugged on his coat until he turned impatiently.

"Where is this boat going?"

"Boat?" He blew out his breath with annoyance. "This is no boat, sonny. This is a Queen of the Sea. She's a ship and she just got in."

"Just in," I repeated dejectedly. "I need a ship that is going to Belgium."

The porter started his cart rolling again. As he moved away he motioned his head to the left. "Might try down there. There are a couple of departures this morning."

"Oh, thank you, sir," I shouted, starting off again with Sukie and Alex in tow.

The second ship was just as frantic and busy as the first. I wondered how they sorted everyone

Through the whirling snow we could see a ship.

out. Men in uniforms scurried back and forth and passengers wandered from ship to land as if they were unsure of which direction they wanted to take.

"Where are you going?" I shouted to a passing porter over the din around us.

"Stateroom Ten," he replied.

"No, no," I shouted, running after him. "Where is the ship going?"

"Hong Kong," he replied, turning a swift corner and disappearing into the crowd.

"Did he say King Kong?" Alex asked as I turned back to herd the kids to the next pier. Finally I had to stop running and slow down to a brisk walk. A funny hard pain had come in my chest and I had to breathe carefully around it.

The sky was too overcast to see where the sun was but I knew that it was at least noon. I kept thinking about the warm kitchen at home and the apple beignets getting staler and staler there on that plate on the table. I blew on my fingers to warm them as we started dejectedly toward the third big ship.

She was huge and beautiful and now I knew better than to call such a craft a boat. Flags rippled above her like kites on a network of bright strings. It seemed impossible but the confusion was even worse than at the other two piers. I struggled like anything to get close to the gangplank.

There were chests everywhere, it seemed to me, and naturally every one looked like Ilsa's. We wove through a maze of steamer trunks and piles of plaid luggage. The crowd was so thick that I could only see the people right beside me. I just knew that if I could fly up and look down I would find Ilsa milling somewhere close to me.

At last I caught up with a porter.

"Where is this ship going?" I asked in a shout.

The man turned and glared at me. Just as he opened his mouth to reply the most horrendous sound I have ever heard filled the air. The ship's whistle trembled the dock beneath our feet and for a moment all my teeth ached. When the sound stopped the porter was gone and people were rushing faster and faster and saying things under their breath like, "Let's go," "Got to go," and "All aboard." Nobody seemed to hear my shouts.

"Please, sir, please," I begged as one man after another pushed by me. Finally I caught at a man's arm. "Where is this ship going, sir?" I asked as loud as I dared.

"Holland," the man said hastily. "But hurry. All aboard."

Holland. I stood very still and shut my eyes. I

could see my geography book and the picture was on the left-hand page. England was a big ink blot leaking out into the channel. Then there was Holland, laced with blue canals. Nestled against it was Belgium.

I opened my eyes with a snap and started running for the ship. "This is it, kids," I shouted. "This one has to be it."

We were all three running when the great whistle sounded again. Only then did the people begin to move with some sort of order. They lined the decks of the ship above me and started waving handkerchiefs and bouquets at the people left on the dock. The last of the passengers were hurrying up the gangplank, some of them crying and looking back as they trotted along.

"We are too late," I whispered out loud. "We have gotten here too late. How could we ever find Ilsa in such a crowd?"

But Alex and Sukie began calling at the top of their lungs. "Ilsa! Pitchou!" they shouted at the crowds lining the ship's deck. "Ilsa! Pitchou!"

Then I saw her. She seemed very short, wedged in between the two tall men who stood beside her. But that pointed nose and those scarlet cheeks could belong to no one but Ilsa.

"Ilsa. Ilsa," I screamed, jumping up and down and shouting. "Ilsa, Ilsa, come back."

Even as we leaped and shouted the great whistle blew again. But Ilsa had seen us. She waved with both arms in the air so that Pitchou's cage waggled crazily back and forth. I could see that Pitchou was barking furiously even though the sound was lost in the great hubbub of noise. Ilsa was being jostled all around and the birdcage suddenly looked very flimsy. I was horrified. What if the cage should break and poor Pitchou be thrown loose in that crowd?

The awful, wonderful idea struck me just like that, with a jolt like the last blast of the ship's whistle.

The men in uniform were all around the gangplank now, sorting out the people and helping to keep the crowds back.

"Wait here," I ordered Sukie and Alex. "Whatever happens, wait right here."

I ran toward the gangplank full speed. One officer grabbed at me as I passed, shouting, "Hey, there, boy." I only shook off his hand and kept dodging and running.

My mind was racing. How could I be sure to get Pitchou out of that cage? If Pitchou were off the ship, Ilsa would never go away and leave him. I had to get Pitchou to run down that gangplank, one way or another.

****

Pitchou

At the top of the gangplank the largest officer of all was directing the passengers. His smile was almost as shiny as the braid on his coat. He was motioning in the air with a small black stick as if he were a bandmaster leading an orchestra.

The stick. Perhaps Pitchou might confuse it with his own black stick. If I could catch Pitchou's eye and throw the stick back to shore, Pitchou would follow—with Ilsa right behind.

Just as I darted past the man, I grabbed at the officer's stick. It didn't come loose at once as I had hoped. When I had it firmly, I understood why. It had been fastened to the man's wrist with a short leather loop.

He shouted after me. "Stop that crazy kid. Stop that boy." I was close to Ilsa by then. She was hurrying toward me with a worried frown and the birdcage flopping every which way as Pitchou bounced drunkenly around inside.

I held up the officer's stick and shouted very loud.

"Fetch, Pitchou. Fetch." Then I threw the stick back down the gangplank into the crowd where Suki and Alex were waiting.

Pitchou gave one sharp bark as he lunged against the side of the birdcage. I didn't have to open it. The wicker bars snapped at his weight and he flew toward the ground like a black shadow. Ilsa called after him in a wail, "Come back, Pitchou, come back."

It was no use. I darted down the gangplank at Pitchou's heels and Ilsa teetered uncertainly there at the top before starting again—down the gangplank behind us. The ship's whistle sounded for that one last time. Pitchou, his pink tongue trailing along in the air, ran down the ramp among the people's feet, toppling them like tenpins. The largest officer of all sat down the hardest, *whoof*ing as he went. A porter who swerved his cart to miss Pitchou sent luggage streaming across the gang-

146

plank into a barrier that no one could pass.

"Oliver. Oliver," I heard Ilsa call. I looked back just in time to see a man topple against her. The birdcage swayed in her hand and she lost her hold on it. It tumbled into the water to bob along like a lacy cork.

I felt myself being caught by all manner of angry hands. "Here he is." "I have the rascal." "What is the matter with the little beast?" a dozen voices clattered at me. Someone hauled me by the collar to the officer whose stick I had grabbed. The man dangled me like a puppet before the officer's red-dened face.

"You—you—" The officer couldn't find words bad enough to say to me. "My stick—you—"

Before the officer caught his breath, Ilsa was there. Her gray hat was askew and her face was scarlet but she seized me and folded me tight against her stout stomach. "Is very good boy," she told the officer firmly. "Is all a big mistake."

I felt something warm against my leg. Pitchou was smiling up at me with that wrinkledy monkey face. Between his legs lay the officer's stick.

I knelt and picked up the stick and handed it to the officer.

"Your stick, sir," I said as politely as I could. "I

am sorry I borrowed it without your permission."

"SORRY," the officer shouted, grabbing the stick. I thought for one awful minute that he was going to beat me with it right there. Instead he looked past me and his mouth got twitchy the way Dad's sometimes does. Then he grinned and began to shake with laughter, rich full laughter that warmed the cold winter air.

A murmuring began behind me and other people began to chuckle and then to laugh. I glanced back and understood why.

A lady was now wearing her flowered hat around her neck like a Hawaiian lei. Two gentlemen with proper suits and striped vests were wearing hats squashed and flat like circus clowns. A beautiful umbrella had been caught on the porter's cart so that he looked like a Good Humor man selling plaid luggage instead of ice cream.

"Boys," said one of the gentlemen in the striped vests, ramming his fist into his hat to make it tall again, "are still boys, I am delighted to say."

There was something nervous about the sound of the ship's whistle, and the officer stopped laughing to turn very brisk.

"Young man, if you are a passenger on this ship, get on. If you are not, and I certainly hope you are

148

not, get lost before I think this all over and lose my temper."

"Yes, sir," I said, backing off with Pitchou in my arms. "I'm not, sir, and thank you very much, sir."

Ilsa followed me, puffing and straining to keep up. It was remarkable how the rest of the people divided themselves into those leaving and those staying behind. By the time I had led Ilsa to Alex and Sukie, the gangplank was up and little tugboats were steaming around the ship.

As we stood there catching our breaths, Alex squealed and pointed at the water. There against the side of the ship right close to us was Pitchou's birdcage, bobbing and slapping in the current.

As I watched the birdcage, I realized that something strange was happening. The door of the cage, which had still been fastened when Pitchou broke through the side, opened as if by an invisible hand. The old blue ball, washed clean by being tumbled around in the cage, floated out on the water, bright as new. Then the stick floated free.

I punched Ilsa in excitement. "The stick," I shouted. "Look at Pitchou's stick."

The carved dark places on the old stick were washed clean, and in those crevices you could see the glow of many colors . . . red like ruby, a blue

with a single eye like a sapphire. . . . Jewels set
into the carved design of the small black stick.

"The wand," Ilsa said in a hushed voice. "The
stick of Pitchou is the magic wand of the faeries."

Then suddenly, as if by magic, the wand disappeared. It didn't sink and there was no hand there
to seize it. It was simply there one minute and gone

the next, like the poltergeist and the doppleganger and the shabby old elf.

"You're free," I shouted, jumping up and down and hugging her. "That was what they wanted all the time. That is what they were pestering you about. Pitchou had their magic wand, and now you can stay with us forever."

"Why didn't they just take it away from Pitchou and save everybody all this bother?" Sukie asked.

"Did you ever try to take that stick away from Pitchou?" Alex asked her back.

Ilsa laughed. The people were waving from the ship and all of us waved back. "Bon voyage. Bon voyage," we shouted, right along with the other people there on the dock.

"There are apple ben-yays at home," Alex reminded us wistfully.

With one last glance at the birdcage bobbing bleakly out to sea, Ilsa and Sukie and Alex and I turned to start back home.

We had to use Ilsa's money to take a cab because we only had fourteen cents left, and one of them was an Indian penny Miss Floss had won in a contest and given me to save forever.

"I'm really ashamed of myself," Sukie admitted

in the back of the cab. "I should have *known* that wasn't a real poltergeist or doppelganger or genuine shabby old elf. They were all done wrong, you know. The poltergeist was not even destructive. The doppelganger used dead people instead of live ones, and the elf was simply a disgrace. In the end it was Oliver who got their stick away from Pitchou. The faeries didn't do it at all."

Ilsa stared at her a moment. "The faeries is very old and science very new. Is maybe the faeries don't know science like you do. Maybe another time they do better."

I glanced over to see if she was teasing Sukie but her expression was perfectly serious. I made it a point not to look at my neat scientist sister. But I wondered if she had as much new respect for things she couldn't prove as I had for her own proven skill at accumulating the proper information for important things like getting us to the ship on time.

****

TWELVE

Hodgepodge

It was good to be home. The snow was melting fast the way the first snow of winter always does. It dripped and chimed outside the kitchen window while Pitchou crunched kibbles from his bowl and the rest of us ate the cold beignets we had been thinking about all day long.

"Is so good to be home," Ilsa said, licking the last of the sugar from her round finger.

"Tell me one more thing," Sukie pressed. "Where did Pitchou get that dreadful wand in the first place?"

Ilsa shook her head. "Is very mysterious. There was picnic. I took fine roasted hen and eels and sausages."

"Did you say eels?" Sukie asked weakly.

"Green eels," Ilsa nodded. "Very tasty. We ate in sunshine and I close my eyes, just for quick winks. I woke to long shadows on the grass and it almost night. Pitchou was by me with mud all over and looking very tired. In his jaws he have that dirty stick he never ever let go of after that."

"Then he must have stolen it from the faeries while you were sleeping." Sukie nodded. "On the day of the great beetle hunt."

"Is very good dog," Ilsa said quickly. "Is was a mistake."

Sukie grinned over at me. "At our house we have only good boys and good dogs. They only make mistakes."

"Is very bad to take a stick from a policeman," Ilsa said, looking at me sternly.

"Is pretty bad to steal a magic wand from the faeries," I reminded her, grinning.

There was hardly any time to do all that needed doing that afternoon. I had to carve a new stick for Pitchou with lots of nice deep ridges in it like the one he lost. Sukie had to help scrape carrots and peel potatoes because Ilsa was so very late in getting dinner started. Alex had to go upstairs and check on Teddy, and managed to fall asleep while he was up there.

Mom stopped at the door with a gasp.

"My goodness, something smells good in here," she called.

"Hochepot," Ilsa explained. "Sukie help me make it."

"Hodgepodge?" I asked.

"Is very close." Ilsa laughed. "Is beef and onion and potato and carrots . . ."

"Enough, enough." Mom laughed too, hanging her coat away and handing Dad a hanger for his. "I am starving already."

"Speaking of hodgepodge," Dad said, "the snow caused traffic problems all over town. The late edition of the paper carried a story about some mischievous little boy who delayed the departure of an ocean liner. And the traffic department had to tow away a pushcart that was left at the pier. What a day."

"What a day indeed," Mom agreed, lifting the lid of the pot to take a deep smell of the soup. "I have such exciting news for everyone that I almost called you at school to tell you."

I saw Sukie's eyes roll upward at the relief of that "almost."

"I had a phone call from Miss Floss. It seems that she has won another contest—an Australian cooking contest with the recipe for that wonderful fresh ham she bakes in a crust. And a local millionaire has offered to help her start a restaurant there, which is another dream we didn't even know she had."

We were all staring at Mom as she continued. "Poor Miss Floss, she was so tempted, but she wouldn't consider the man's offer until she heard that we were doing all right here."

"Of course you told her to stay," I said hopefully.

She nodded. "Yes, I did, Oliver. It was so plain that it was something she wanted to do. Then I remembered. Ilsa, do you still think maybe you'll just have to leave us and move on?"

Ilsa glanced at Pitchou, who was guarding his new stick with careful paws. Then she shook her head. "Is not even possible that I will ever leave unless you sent me."

"That's a relief," Dad said happily.

Then he glanced up with a puzzled frown. "There's that funny noise we used to have. That bumping from upstairs."

I must have frozen as Sukie and Ilsa and I stared at each other, wide eyed. Then we ran into the hall and saw him. Alex, wakened from his nap, was bumping down the stairs on his bottom, too sleepy to stand up and walk. In back of him bumped Teddy, just one step behind.

"Look at my sleepyhead," Mom crooned, reaching for him.

He crawled on her lap with his eyes still half shut.

"I think I had a dream," he mumbled. "About Ilsa and Pitchou and the faeries." Then he sniffed and his eyes flew wide. "Something smells good. Let's eat."

"Hodgepodge," Ilsa said, pronouncing it Mom's way.

Sukie started laughing the same minute I did. I didn't want to laugh that hard but I couldn't help it. I guess it was what they call hysterical laughter.

Mom gave us both a funny look as she rocked Alex back and forth. "I didn't think it was *that* funny," she said in a sort of injured tone.

"Hungry people laugh funny," Alex said, shutting his eyes and leaning back against her with a sigh.

ABOUT THE AUTHOR

Mary Francis Shura has written nineteen books for young people. Born in Kansas, not far from Dodge City, the author has lived in many parts of the United States, including California and Massachusetts. Both of her parents came from early settler families of Missouri.

Aside from writing fiction for young readers and adults, Mary Francis Shura enjoys tennis, chess, reading, and cooking—especially making bread.

The author is married and the mother of a son, Dan, and three daughters, Minka, Ali, and Shay. She currently makes her home in the western suburbs of Chicago, in the village of Willowbrook.

ABOUT THE ARTIST

Bertram M. Tormey is noted for his portraiture of people and dogs. He has traveled extensively in France, studying the Old Masters and particularly the Impressionists. He lives in Katonah, New York.